Praise for the work of Alicia Gael

Murder on Castaway Island

Good book! This book had a bit of everything! It had suspense, action packed, intrigue, mystery, murder, revenge, a great who done it, great plot twist, and some crazy twists and turns!

-Debbie B., *NetGalley*

I didn't count how many times I had to remind myself to breathe. I was on the edge of my seat almost from page one and only sat back comfortably after I'd read the last sentence.

-Jude S., *NetGalley*

This is like a modern day Agatha Christie. A well written fast paced, engaging and entertaining mystery. This will have you guessing who did it until the end. Well done Alicia Gael.

-Bonnie K., *NetGalley*

The author did a superb job of developing each character, so they were three-dimensional with their own unique voices, and how Alicia Gael transitioned from the multiple perspectives was perfect. This was a great, quick read that I highly recommend.

-Amy D., *NetGalley*

MURDER, MAYHEM
AND SEX ON THE BEACH

Other Bella Books by Alicia Gael

Murder on Castaway Island

About the Author

I started writing in the sixth grade on my dad's manual typewriter. I made up sweet romance stories (at twelve was there any other kind?) for my friends, featuring them and their celebrity crushes falling in love. By the time I was in middle school, sports had become my passion, and I put the typewriter back in the closet. As I got older, life and earning a paycheck moved to the top of the list, and I didn't write again until I was in my midtwenties. Over the next thirty-five years, I wrote over a dozen first chapters that never went anywhere except into a file cabinet.

After college, I didn't know what I wanted to do, so I drifted from job to job. I delivered for Domino's, made pizzas at Me & Eds and Round Table, flipped burgers at Jack in the Box, and worked in retail. I was also a preschool teacher and a school bus driver, then a juvenile hall counselor, which led to my first full-time job as a probation officer. I was twenty-eight years old, and I remember thinking, *who in their right mind would give me a badge, handcuffs, and a gun and send me out on my own?* I went on to arrest hundreds of people over the next twenty years without shooting a single one, not even the Chihuahua who chased me onto the hood of a car or the two pit bulls that snuck up behind me and almost made me pee my pants.

At forty, I enrolled at CSU Fresno. I earned a master's degree in criminology, which led to teaching part-time at the College of Sequoias in Visalia, California. I left the probation department in 2007 and became a full-time, tenured professor.

In October 2018, the local public library hosted a pre-NANOWRIMO workshop. That four-hour workshop kicked off my journey to become a writer. At the age of 62, I earned a creative writing certificate from the UC San Diego Extension program; published three poems in the Ezine, *For Women Who Roar*; a flash piece in *The Bangalore Review* (Deception); and a short story in *The Quiet Reader* (No Time For Stories). Also, the first chapter of my unfinished historical fiction novel, *The Journey*, was published in The California Writer's Club 2022 Review.

In November of 2021, I completed my first NANOWRIMO. That 50K words became my first novel, *Murder on Castaway Island*. Two years later it was published by Bella Books.

I retired from teaching in May 2023. It feels like my life has come full circle, I'm finally doing the two things I've always wanted to do; be a full-time writer and live near the ocean. When not writing, you can find me kayaking, reading (I average 100 books a year), learning to play the ukulele, or drinking Prosecco with my wife, Donna.

You can contact me on my website: www.aliciagael.com
Facebook: aliciagaelwrites
Instagram and Threads: aliciagael_writes
Email: aliciagaelwrites@gmail.com

Bella Books, Inc.
P.O. Box 10543
Tallahassee, FL 32302

First Edition - 2025

Editor: Ann Roberts

ISBN: 978-1-64247-620-0

PUBLISHER'S NOTE

Acknowledgments

I'm reluctant to write an acknowledgements page, knowing that I'll inevitably forget to thank someone and later realize I've forgotten to thank them, and I'll feel terrible. So if you are the somebody I forgot to thank, just know that I feel terrible and beg you to forgive me for the oversight. Please be assured that your support has meant the world to me.

First, I need to thank Linda and Jessica Hill, and everyone at Bella Books who had a hand in getting this book published. I am eternally grateful you took a chance on me.

The wonderful Ann Roberts, editor and author extraordinaire. Your patience and guidance have made me a better writer and this a better book.

My crack team of beta readers, Susanne, Erin, Toni and Donna. Thank you for taking the time to point out all my mistakes.

The GCLS Writing Academy 1and 2 ('23 and '24) classmates, especially my 'pod people' Kate Pringle, Lana P. and Mila McKay for your love, encouragement and support. I know we'll be friends for life.

My WA1 mentor, Lynette Beers, who went way beyond what was expected and edited the whole book before I submitted it to Bella. Lynette, thank you, thank you, thank you and I owe you hours and hours of beta reading whenever you need it.

Lastly, my wife, Donna, who loves me unconditionally even when I'm a pain in the…

Dedication

To the little girl who wanted to be a writer but was afraid to try. Dreams do come true.

MURDER, MAYHEM
AND SEX ON THE BEACH

Alicia Gael

BELLA
BOOKS

CHAPTER ONE

It's never a good day when your car is stolen right outside your house, and the thief leads the cops on a high-speed chase and then crashes said car into a septic truck. It's even worse when your car is a county probation vehicle, and your boss doesn't have a sense of humor.

My name is Riley Reynolds. I've worked at the San Luis Obispo (SLO) County Probation Department for four years. Currently, I'm assigned to the warrant apprehension unit. It's my job to track down rogue probationers and drag them before the court so they can explain to a judge why they violated their terms of probation. Sounds easy enough, right? The thing is most wayward probationers don't want to appear in court because they face having their probation status revoked and their prison sentence imposed. It can make for some tricky situations. Like the one I was currently in.

It was a gorgeous September day. There was barely a breeze and not a cloud in the sky. I'd stopped by my apartment for lunch when my on-again, off-again girlfriend, Tate Walker, a detective in the property crimes unit of the SLO Police Department, called. She was laughing.

Tate and I had been seeing each other for a couple of years. No promises had been made, we hadn't moved in together, and there were no plans to rent a U-Haul. I'll be honest with you, I'm the one holding things up. There were three reasons: first, I had been almost engaged to be married but ended up with a broken heart. Her name was Michelle. We'd lived together our senior year of college. I'd planned a romantic trip to the coast for spring break and planned to pop the question. I bought a ring and everything. On the Friday before the trip, I skipped class to pack and walked in on her screwing her best friend with a dildo. To add insult to injury, she'd always claimed she wasn't into toys.

The second reason was kids; Tate wanted them, I didn't. It's not really an issue you can compromise on. It's not that I didn't like kids. They were fine as long as they were somebody else's. My office partner, Patty, was expecting, and I was excited for her. I'd be happy to babysit and buy toys that made a lot of noise and would drive her crazy. But I'd be even happier to hand them back at the end of the day.

The third reason was my plan to become an FBI Special Agent. I'd missed the filing deadline twice. The first time because my father had a heart attack and needed open heart surgery. It hadn't been a good time to pick up and move across the country. The following year I was so busy at work I forgot to submit my application. I was bound and determined to submit it this year.

But back to the story. I was standing in my kitchen making a Gouda and tomato sandwich, not just any Gouda, mind you, it was Irish Gouda. Yes, I'm a cheese snob. There isn't any of that cheap processed shit in my refrigerator. To be honest, there isn't much of anything in my refrigerator. I keep forgetting to go to the grocery store, so I end up eating takeout a lot. Anyway, just as I placed the second slice of tomato on my sandwich, the phone rang. Tate's name appeared on the screen, and I pictured her naked body against mine in the shower that morning.

"Hi, babe, what's up?" I could hear sirens in the distance, but I live near a busy street, so sirens aren't unusual.

"Riles, please tell me you know where your probation car is right now."

I took a bite out of my sandwich and walked to the window. "Yeah, it's in front of…Oh, fuck, it's gone." I dropped the sandwich and ran for the door and down the stairs. "What the hell, Tate?" I scanned the street in both directions.

"Shit, Riles, did you lock it?"

"Of course, I locked it! I'm not an idiot." I racked my brain, trying to remember if, in fact, I had locked it.

"I know you're not, but half a dozen cops are chasing it down the highway."

I knew by the sound of her voice she was shaking her head. This wasn't the first time something ludicrous had happened to me.

"I'll call you back when we have them in custody, hopefully before they wreck it," she said, then hung up.

Crap, crap, crap. My boss was going to kill me. Luckily my Glock 9mm was attached to my hip and not locked in the trunk, and I hadn't left any important files in the back seat. Dreading the conversation, I dialed his office. The phone rang one time.

"Stevenson," he said without preamble.

I took a deep breath, hopefully not my last one as a probation officer. "Hi, Stan. I've got a problem."

"Yeah? What now? Lost your keys? Dropped your pepper spray in the toilet?"

"That only happened once," I protested. "And this is a little more serious than that."

"Out with it, Reynolds. I don't have all day."

I could picture the stack of warrant files waiting to be assigned, at least two cold cups of coffee, and empty Snickers wrappers on his desk. He was fifty-five, rarely ate anything healthy, and was at least forty pounds overweight. He was a heart attack waiting to happen.

"I just got a call from SLO PD. My car's been stolen, and they're in pursuit," I blurted out as fast as I could.

A second passed, then another. "When you say *your* car, you mean that blue piece of shit you drive, right?"

I stretched my neck from side to side. "I wish it were, Stan, I really wish it were. Unfortunately, the goddesses are not on my side today."

I heard a loud thud and pictured Stan pounding the desk with the heel of his hand. "Goddamn it, Reynolds, how did this happen?"

Like an answer to a prayer, my personal phone rang, and Tate's name popped up on the screen. "Stan, the police are on my other phone. I'll call you back." I hung up before he could get another word out.

"Tate, did they catch him?"

"Riles, I've got good news, and I've got bad news."

"Shit, shit, shit." I hated good news, bad news scenarios.

"You're not far off."

"What the hell does that mean?"

"Well, the good news is we stopped her."

I rolled my eyes and looked at the ceiling. "Her?"

"Yeah, it was a chick with pink hair. But she got away."

"Is that the bad news?"

"Well, there's bad news, and then there's bad, bad news."

"Just tell me, I'm already up shit creek. How bad can it be?"

"There was a small accident, but no one was injured."

"Okay. What's the really bad news?"

"She ran into the back of a septic truck, and your car is covered in shit." I could tell she was trying hard not to laugh. "So yeah, it's shit creek."

CHAPTER TWO

An hour later, Tate picked me up at home and dropped me off at my office to face my fate. I took a deep breath, squared my shoulders, and walked into Stan's office. He looked up as he snapped the lid closed on a jumbo container of antacids. He popped a handful in his mouth like they were candy. I shifted my weight from one foot to the other.

"The car's salvageable. Lucky for you, the windows were rolled up. But the vents were open, so there's a smell. It's going to cost the department a bundle to clean it," he said. "And no one's ever gonna want to drive it, so consider it permanently assigned to you for as long as you work here. Which is in question right now."

My eyebrows shot up, and my jaw dropped.

"There will be an investigation. If it's determined that you left the car unlocked, there will be disciplinary action. Most likely a demotion."

"Fu...Fudge," I said through clenched teeth. "Stan, I swear I locked the doors."

He shrugged. "It's out of my hands, Reynolds. The chief went off like a cherry bomb in a bucket. It wasn't pretty."

"Should I go talk to him?"

"Hell no. You should stay far away from him and off his radar until the investigation is done."

I plopped down in the WWII-era metal chair in front of his Cold War-era desk. "Okay." I ran my fingers through my hair and reminded myself to get a haircut. "Do they know who stole it?"

"Does the name Patricia Higgins ring a bell?"

Fuck. Of course, it was Pinky. "Yeah, it rings a big bell."

Stan's phone rang. He turned his back to me and grunted into the phone, then turned back around and typed something into his computer. When he was done typing, he looked at me and scowled.

I looked over his shoulder at the tree outside his window. A few leaves had begun to turn yellow, and soon they'd be a brilliant shade of orange. Fall would be here before long.

I stretched my neck from side to side as I waited for Stan to get off the phone. I could hear whoever was on the other end mention Pinky's name. I stared at the ceiling. Pinky was the first kid I'd processed when I worked at Juvenile Hall. She'd been seventeen, but it wasn't the first time she'd been arrested. That had been when she was fourteen. She'd been brought in for car theft, and it wasn't her first car theft. That had been when she was twelve.

It was also the same day Tate pulled me over for speeding and asked for my phone number. It was the first day at my new job, and I was running late. When I turned right off Monterey onto Santa Rosa Street, red lights flashed in my rearview mirror, and the high-pitched squeal of a motorcycle cop's siren pierced the air. I pulled to the curb and turned off the engine. I'd glanced in the rearview mirror and watched the cop pull in behind me, dismount, and then pull off their helmet.

It was Tate, and she was even sexier than she'd been in high school. In fact, she was hot as hell. The tight-fitting motorcycle pants tucked into knee-high black boots and a black short-sleeved uniform T-shirt that fit her like a glove.

Seeing her took me back the heated kiss in the high school locker room all those years ago. I was a junior, and she was a senior. It was after the last game of the season. Everyone else had left and it was just the two of us. She had smiled and taken a step toward me.

"Riley, the way you look at me drives me crazy." She wet her lips with the tip of her tongue. "Can I kiss you?"

I couldn't speak. I nodded and she cupped my jaw with her hand and touched her lips to mine. My heart rate tripled. I spread my lips and let her in. My knees buckled when her tongue caressed mine and I grabbed onto her waist to hold myself up. The kiss didn't last nearly long enough. She pulled away but kept her hand on my jaw. "That was nice," she whispered. I couldn't speak, she'd rocked my world. "Thank you, Riley Reynolds." She winked and flashed me a devilish grin and walked out of the locker room.

I'd replayed that kiss over and over in my head for months. I wanted more, but that was it, Tate never kissed me again. For the rest of the school year it was as if the kiss never happened.

Looking in my side mirror, I watched her walk up to my window. I may have drooled a little bit. She tapped her knuckles on my window, and I pushed the button to lower it.

"Hello, officer," I said, trying not to stare.

She didn't say anything for what seemed like an hour, then pulled off her aviator sunglasses. Her blue eyes sparkled, and her lips curved into a smile. "Well, well, well. You're back."

"Yes, I've been back for several months." I smiled. "It's my first day at a new job, and I don't want to be late. So can we hurry this up?" When our eyes met, lightning shot through me and down to a place that hadn't seen any action in quite a while.

She flashed that brilliant smile at me. Her perfect teeth were even whiter than I'd remembered. "Sure." She took a small notebook and pen from her chest pocket and held it out. "Name and phone number, please." Her right eyebrow arched.

I reached for the pen. Heat raced up my arm and down to my center when our fingers touched. A picture of those fingers touching me everywhere and filling me with pleasure flashed in my head. My heart raced. "My phone number?"

"So I can call you." She flashed that same devilish smile she had in high school.

"You want to call me?" I almost stuttered.

She put her hands in the pockets of her tight-fitting pants. "Yes. I would like to call you."

My mind spun. I wasn't looking for a girlfriend. I had a plan, and it didn't include getting serious with someone and ending up with a broken heart when I eventually went to the FBI academy. Could we keep things casual? I wanted Tate Walker like I wanted air to breathe. I wanted to feel her arms around me, her lips on mine, our bodies grinding together. Maybe Tate wasn't interested in anything serious either. Maybe we could keep things casual, with no commitments. I could do that.

I glanced at the clock on the dashboard. I had ten minutes to get to work. I smiled at her then jotted down my number. "Okay. I'm on swing shift for the next three months."

"Where do you work?"

"The Probation Department. I'll be at Juvenile Hall to start. But I won't be if I don't get there in the next ten minutes."

She put the pen and notebook back in her chest pocket. "Okay, you are free to go, ma'am. Please watch your speed from now on."

Stan's gravelly voice brought me back to reality. "Higgins has an outstanding warrant for failure to report to her probation officer." His eyes bulged out a little bit. I hoped he didn't have a heart attack while I was still in his office. The thought of giving him CPR made me queasy. "Find her and book her ass in jail." I could tell he was trying not to yell, but several heads turned toward us.

I stood. "Okay, Stan. I'm on it."

"I mean it, Riley. Find her before she steals another car and causes any more mayhem." He picked up the cold cup of coffee,

took a drink, and spit it back into the cup. "Shit!" He glared up at me. "What are you still doing here? Get out of my office."

"I'll go talk to Pinky's mother." I turned to leave. "She may know where she's hiding."

He didn't look up from the file he'd opened. "Fine."

"We'll take Patty's vehicle." Patty Painter was my office partner. We were the modern-day versions of Cagney and Lacey if Cagney and Lacey had been probation officers rather than cops. Of course, I was Cagney.

"What? No!" He slammed the file closed, his face turning the color of a pomegranate.

"We can't take her vehicle?"

"I don't care what car you take. She stays in the office."

I almost laughed. "Stan, she's pregnant, not disabled."

"I don't care. She stays here."

I crossed my arms. "Stan, this could be construed as discrimination."

He stood, put his fists on the desk, and leaned toward me. "Fine," he growled. "If anything happens to her, I'll hold you responsible."

I swallowed. "We're only going to 7-Eleven. That's where Pinky's mom works. We'll see what she knows and be back before you know it."

He looked skeptical. "Fine. Just remember what I said."

"I absolutely will." I backed out of his office and wondered if he really cared about Patty's safety or if he didn't want to deal with the shitstorm that would occur if a pregnant officer was injured on duty.

Thirty minutes later, Patty and I pulled into the 7-Eleven on the corner of Marsh and Broad Streets. Lena Higgins had Pinky when she was only sixteen years old. She was thirty-seven now but looked more like an older sister than the mom of a twenty-one-year-old.

When we walked in, Lena was placing hot dogs on the grill behind the register. She looked up when the bell buzzed over the door. When she saw me, she glanced up at the ceiling, blew out a breath, and looked back at me. "What's she done now?"

I rested my hands on my gun belt. Did I mention that probation officers in SLO County are armed? It's a pretty controversial thing. On the one hand, probation officers are a lot like social workers. We try to rehabilitate people and get them on the right track. On the other hand, we're peace officers with the power to arrest anyone on probation. Sometimes those people don't want to be arrested, and they put up a fight. Sometimes they have guns of their own and aren't afraid to use them. It's a mixed bag.

"She stole my probation car, led the police on a high-speed chase, then crashed it."

"Into the back of a septic truck, no less," Patty chimed in, trying not to laugh.

I gave her the stink eye.

Lena rested her fists on her hips and looked at the floor. "I tried with that girl. Really, I tried." She looked up at me. "Riley, you know I've tried. She's just like her father."

Pinky's father was Tommy Higgins, a three-time loser now serving ten years for burglary and identity theft.

"I know you tried, Lena. I'll do what I can to keep Pinky from going to prison. But she has to turn herself in. If the cops find her first, you know she'll resist, which will make things a whole lot worse."

"I know. I know."

"Do you have any idea where she's staying? Any friends that would hide her?"

"Try her girlfriend's. Her name's Trixie something, maybe Adams. She lives in the green-and-white house across from the prep school."

The Mission College Preparatory was the Catholic high school. It's where the wealthy people in town sent their kids. Obviously, it wasn't where Tate or I had gone. San Luis Obispo High School had been good enough for us, and since it was free, it fit our parents' budgets.

Lena continued to talk as she pulled a sack of hot dog buns out from under the counter. "She's also asked me to drop her off a couple of times at a house on Pismo Street, next to Planned Parenthood. I don't have any idea who lives there."

"Thanks, Lena. We'll do our best to find her before the cops do." I opened the door and paused. "You'll let us know if you hear from her?"

Lena nodded. "I've still got your card."

Back in the car, Patty stretched the seatbelt over her ever-expanding tummy. Being pregnant looked really uncomfortable, and it reinforced my lack of desire to have kids.

"School's getting out soon." Patty snapped the belt into place. "Maybe we try the house on Pismo first?"

"Good plan." I put the car in drive and pulled onto Broad Street. "I could use an iced coffee. How about you?"

"As long as it's decaf. I don't need the baby awake all night," Patty said as she rubbed a hand over her large baby bump.

"Linnaega's is close."

"Perfect, I've been craving a peanut butter cookie, and theirs are the best."

Traffic was light as I pulled onto Higuera. I found an empty parking spot on the one-way street across from Bubblegum Alley, and pulled in. Bubblegum Alley is practically a historical landmark in SLO. The ten-foot high, seventy-foot-long alley is covered in every color and flavor of gum known to man. It started in the 1950s as a rivalry between SLO High School students and Cal Poly students trying to outdo each other. It's been stripped and cleaned twice over the past decades. The last attempt in the 1990s was met with resistance by the locals and the city hasn't tried again since.

"I'll go." Patty undid her seatbelt and opened the door. "I need to walk."

I sat in the car and watched people casually stroll down Higuera. With its eclectic shops, restaurants, breweries, and proximity to Mission San Luis Obispo de Tolosa, it was a popular area for students and tourists. The vibe in this part of town is pretty chill and today was no different. It was a warm autumn afternoon, several groups of high school students walked by, trying to look like they were college students, and college students walked by, ignoring the high school students. Tourists strolled past, glancing in the shops and looking over restaurant menus posted near the entrances of the establishments. So, when a very muscular, bald-headed guy ran out of the alley, it caught my attention. He skidded to a stop when he saw the probation car then took off up Higuera like his ass was on fire, almost running into Patty on her way back. Luckily, she wasn't jostled much, and our iced coffees weren't in any danger.

When she got to the car she handed me a coffee through the window. "What the hell was that do you suppose?" she asked as she climbed back inside.

"Beats me." I slid a straw into my iced coffee and glanced toward the alley. There was smoke billowing out of it. "Shit, there's a fire." I put my coffee in the cup holder and opened the door. "Call 911."

I looked to my left to make sure there wasn't any oncoming traffic and ran toward the alley. A couple of people ran out, coughing. Just inside the alley, there was an industrial-size dumpster on fire. I breathed a sigh of relief that the wall behind it was brick, so the building wasn't in immediate danger. I exited the alley as sirens blared, and a fire engine rounded the corner at Chorro Street and stopped in front of the alley. Men and women in khaki firefighting gear jumped out of the truck and began pulling hoses from the back end. I identified myself to the commander and told her about the man I saw running from the alley just before the fire started. She asked me to wait for the police and give them my statement. I walked back to the car and leaned against it. Patty handed me my iced coffee, pulled a cookie from the small white bag, and took a bite. "Do you think it was the guy that ran into me?"

"Probably. He came running out of the alley like the hounds of hell were chasing him."

I sipped my iced coffee as a black-and-white police SUV pulled up next to the fire engine. The driver's side door opened, and Tate stepped out. Damn, she looked good. The black low-rise jeans showed off her ass, the ass I'd had my hands all over last night, and the teal-colored blazer she wore to hide her service weapon hugged her narrow waist and broad shoulders.

Patty elbowed me in the ribs. "Easy, tiger," she laughed.

"What?"

"I can hear your libido from here." She took a sip of her coffee. "And you need to wipe your mouth."

"What? Why?"

"You're drooling."

"I am not."

She put her hand on my shoulder. "You can deny it all you want, Riley. But you've got it bad for her."

"No, I don't."

"Says the woman who needs to wipe drool from her chin."

"I'm not drooling." I ran the back of my hand across my mouth, just in case.

Tate waved and then headed over to the fire captain. Her spiky bedhead blond hair looked just as sexy as it had when she'd stepped out of my shower this morning. She looked back at me and winked. Damn it, I was going to have to swing by the house and change into a dry pair of underwear. As often as I ran into Tate at work, I should be keeping an extra pair in my desk.

"Riley." Patty snapped her fingers in front of my face. "Riley. Snap out of it."

I pushed away from the car and tossed my jacket in the back seat. Even though we were parked in the shade, I was suddenly hot. "What? I'm fine." I needed to get a grip. There was no way my relationship with Tate was going to get any more serious than it already was. Our friends-with-benefits arrangement was working just fine.

Tate and the captain talked for a few minutes, then shook hands. Tate turned around and walked back across the street, her eyes laser focused on mine. I slid my sunglasses on and took a sip of my coffee. The pounding in my chest might have been so loud that it gave me away. I leaned back against the car again and crossed one ankle over the other.

"Officers." She winked at me then turned to Patty. "How's the baby?"

"Kicking the shit out of my bladder." She rubbed her belly. "Can we hurry this up? I've got to get to a bathroom, or it won't be pretty."

"Sure." Tate laughed, then turned to me. "The captain said you saw a guy run out of the alley just before the fire started?"

"Yeah. White guy about six feet, two hundred pounds, muscular. Shaved head, white T-shirt, blue jeans." I felt my forehead wrinkle. "There was something on his left forearm."

She took a small notebook from her back pocket and wrote it down. "Tattoo?"

"I don't think so. But I couldn't tell from here."

She returned the notebook to her pocket. "Thanks. I'll give this to dispatch to send out." She smiled at me. "Why don't I come over tonight and take your statement? I'd hate for Patty to leave a puddle right here on the street."

Patty walked around the car to the passenger side. "Great idea. That way, you two can kill two birds with one stone. If you get my drift." She opened the door and climbed in.

I opened my car door and turned to look at Tate. "I should be home around six. After we make a pit stop for Patty, we're checking out a house where Pinky might be hiding out."

Tate cocked her head. "Pinky?"

"Patricia Higgins, the car thief."

"Your car?"

I nodded. I could tell she was trying not to laugh. "Okay. Be careful." She turned and started to walk away, then turned back. "Oh, and, Riley…"

"Yeah," I said, trying not to picture her naked in my bed this morning.

"Be sure you lock the car when you get there." She grinned. "You wouldn't want to lose two in one day."

I could feel my face flush. "Damn it, Tate, I did lock my car. Pinky's a car thief. She knows how to pop a lock in less time than it takes you to tie your shoe."

"Okay, babe. I believe you." She winked and then headed to her car.

I climbed into the driver's seat, put both hands on the steering wheel, and blew out a breath. "I'm never going to live this down, am I?"

"Not in this lifetime," Patty said.

CHAPTER THREE

After a quick stop at the courthouse for Patty to empty her bladder, we pulled up in front of the only house next to the Planned Parenthood building. It was an aging, brown, single-story Craftsman with a saggy roof. As we climbed out of the car, a black BMW with windows tinted so dark they had to be illegal, slowly drove by. Something about it set off my Spidey senses.

A waist-high chain-link fence enclosed the neglected property, maybe to keep the occasional anti-choice protester from trespassing. The yard was all dirt. The grass had long since died, a victim of the ongoing drought. A gopher popped its head out of a hole and watched us enter through the gate. It kept its eye on us as we walked to the front door, which was slightly ajar.

I knocked. "Probation Department, anyone here?" It was silent inside, no television blaring or music playing. I pushed the door open further. "Probation Department, is anyone here?" I yelled.

We waited a few seconds. Patty looked at me. "What do you want to do?"

I shrugged. "The door's open. Maybe this is an exigent circumstance situation." I doubted it was, but what the hell? "Let's stick our heads in and have a quick look."

I pushed the door open all the way with my left hand, my right hand on my weapon just in case. "Probation Department. We're coming in."

I took two steps into the entryway and peeked into the kitchen. *Shit!* There was a body on the floor. "There's a body," I said over my shoulder as I walked to it and knelt. Patty pulled her weapon and held it at the ready.

It didn't look like the guy was breathing, and there was a lot of blood pooled under him. I placed my fingertips on his neck and felt for a pulse. His skin was cold, and I couldn't find a heartbeat. "He's dead." I stood. "Will you call 911 while I check the rest of the house?" I asked as I pulled a pair of rubber gloves out of my pocket and put them on.

"I should know better than to go on calls with you. It never fails. Something bad happens," Patty said as she put her phone to her ear.

What could I say? She wasn't wrong. This was the third dead body I'd stumbled across in the past year. What were the odds? I took out my service weapon, finger off the trigger, pointed it at the ground, and cautiously entered the living room. It had been tossed. The couch had been flipped over and every cushion slashed. Stuffing blanketed the floor like snow. A bookshelf had been pulled from the wall and books lay everywhere. It broke my little bibliophilic heart.

Sirens screamed nearby as I slowly moved from the living room into the hallway. I pushed open the bathroom door and nudged back the shower curtain. No one was hiding there. I released the breath I'd been holding and headed to the bedroom. I poked my head in. A cyclone had blown through and wreaked havoc. Everything in the closet was on the floor. The nightstand and dresser had been dumped. The pillows and mattress were sliced open, and the stuffing was pulled out. I looked under the bed; no one was there. I backed out of the room.

As I returned to the living room, a black-and-white SLO police car screeched to a stop in front of the house. Two uniformed officers climbed out. A second later, a fire engine pulled up behind them, and EMTs began pulling equipment from the truck. They were a little late for the guy on the kitchen floor.

I holstered my weapon and went to the front door. Patty sat on the front steps, her belly sticking out noticeably.

One of the officers, Doug Winters, had been in Tate's class a year ahead of me. He stopped at the bottom of the steps. "Hi, Patty. When ya due?"

"Four weeks." She rubbed her belly. "I'm going on leave next week if that one can be trusted to stay out of trouble while I'm gone." She motioned to me and smiled.

"Hey, I can manage without you for a few months." I motioned for Doug to follow me inside. "I cleared the house. There's no one here but the dead guy." I pointed to the kitchen.

"How many dead bodies does this make?" a familiar voice asked from the doorway.

I frowned. I hadn't heard another car arrive. "Tate, who called you?" She'd taken off the blazer, and her black T-shirt fit like a second skin.

Doug cleared his throat. "I did." He smiled.

I glared at him, then turned to Tate. "I doubt this has anything to do with your arson case."

She shrugged. "Yeah, probably not." She pointed to the dead guy on the floor. "Is he number three or number four?" I could tell she was trying not to laugh.

I crossed my arms and narrowed my eyes. "It's only the third one."

Doug laughed out loud. "The third one this year."

I glared at him then turned back to Tate. "Isn't there some real detective work you could be doing?" I raised an eyebrow. "Like catching an arsonist?"

Tate raised her hands, palms facing me. "Okay, okay. I know when I'm not welcome." She leaned in and kissed me on the cheek. "I'll see you later." She turned to leave. "Watch out, guys," she said to Doug and his partner. "When Riley's around, anything can happen."

"Oh, you know what can happen." I laughed, and she looked back and winked. As she continued to her car, I stood there admiring her ass in those tight-fitting black jeans.

As Tate drove off, another unmarked police vehicle pulled up. Sue Skylar and Bob Cup climbed out. They were homicide detectives. As Tate kindly pointed out, this was the third time I'd come across a dead body, so it wasn't the first time I'd had to interact with them.

"Well, well, well," Bob said when he got to the door, his face flushed from the heat and the extra forty pounds he carried around his middle. "What a surprise. It's Probation Officer Reynolds—again," he said, trying to hold back a laugh. "What's this, the third one this year? And it's only September. Who knows how many there'll be by New Year's." He pushed past me. "You better not have fucked up my crime scene."

Sue shook her head. "Give it a rest, Bob." She smiled at me and shrugged in that *What can I say, he's an idiot* kind of way. "What do ya have for us?"

"I put gloves on, and I didn't touch anything except the dead guy's neck to feel for a pulse." I leaned against the counter. "The front door was open when we got here. The place had been tossed. Whoever killed him was looking for something."

Bob gruffly instructed Doug and the other officer to canvas the neighbors to see if anyone saw anything and then he told the EMTs they could leave. There were people who could benefit from their services, but the guy on the floor wasn't one of them.

Sue walked over to the doorway and smiled down at Patty. "How ya feeling?"

Patty stood and stretched her back. "Not too bad other than my feet are swollen, and these shoes are killing me."

Sue laughed. "Yeah, I've been there." She turned back to me. "What can you tell me about the dead guy?"

"Not much. We got a tip that Pinky Higgins, a probationer, might be here."

"That the one who stole your car?" Bob chuckled.

I crossed my arms. "Yeah, that one." I wanted to add *you asshole* but thought better of it.

Sue knelt to take a closer look at the dead guy. "Any chance she did this?"

I shook my head. "Pinky's a thief, not a killer. And she's tiny. This guy looks like he's, what, five-ten? Maybe two-fifty? I just don't see it." I paused. "Unless he attacked her. Then she'd fight like hell."

Sue stood and took a notebook out of her jacket pocket. "You never know." She wrote something down. "You got an address for Pinky?"

"According to her mother, she bounces around between her house and her girlfriend's place on Palm Street."

Sue handed me the notebook and pen. "Can you write down those addresses for me?"

"Sure." I wrote down the information and handed the notebook back to Sue. "Also, when we pulled up, a black, late-model BMW with dark-tinted windows drove by slowly. Like they were checking us out."

"Did you get a license plate number?" Bob asked.

"No. I think the plate was covered up."

"You think it was covered?"

By his tone I knew he thought I was an idiot. I wanted to give him the finger but I refrained. I didn't want to deal with Stan if it got back to him that I was acting unprofessionally.

"Do you need anything else? It's been a long day, and I need to get Patty back to the office."

Without looking up from the body, Bob said, "Not now, but you'll need to come into the station tomorrow and give a statement."

"Sure." I turned to Sue. "I'll call in the morning." I looked at Patty. "Let's get out of here."

"You in a hurry?" Patty asked as we walked back down the cracked cement path, the gopher watching us again.

"No. Why?"

She opened the car door and got in. "I saw the kiss Tate gave you. Thought you might be in a hurry to get home."

I started the car. "Seriously? It was just a kiss on the cheek. Maybe you're the one who needs to get home to your husband."

"Dave's still on the road. Won't be back for another week." She laid her hand on her belly. "And I'm eight months pregnant."

"I can't believe you'd let a little thing like that get in the way."

"Well, there's also the three kids who have no concept of privacy. Or that Mommy and Daddy need some alone time occasionally."

I laughed and motioned to her stomach. "Obviously, you were able to find some alone time."

"Shut up. We were talking about you, not me."

"I have nothing to talk about."

"Oh, come on. Tate's coming over tonight to 'take your statement.'" She made quotation marks with her index fingers. "Maybe a little role-play?"

I glanced over at her and then back on the road. "Have you lost your mind?"

"What, you've never role-played cops and robbers in the bedroom?"

"Your hormones must be really out of whack." I laughed. "And even if we did, I'd never tell you."

She pouted. "You're no fun."

The rest of the way to the office, I couldn't get the image of Tate and her handcuffs, and what she could use them for, out of my head.

CHAPTER FOUR

I pulled into the driveway between my place and my landlord's, Mike Logan, house. My apartment is over Mike's garage. It's compact—one bedroom, one bath with a tiny kitchen and a living room big enough for a sleeper sofa, a coffee table, and a big-screen TV. The living room window looks out on Albert Drive, which is usually pretty quiet, except on Saturdays during football season when the Cal Poly Mustangs have a home game. Then the street becomes a giant tailgate party.

When I pulled in, Mike was out front watering his award-winning multicolored roses. Mike's a sweetheart, and for some reason, treats me like the daughter he never had. My rent is so cheap it's almost embarrassing, so I don't complain when he cranks up the '80s disco music at eight on a Sunday morning. Mike's a CPA during the week, but on weekends he transforms into drag performer Miss Ivy. From what I've heard, he rakes in the tips. You'd think he'd sleep in on Sundays after performing until two in the morning, but he's always up by seven and often makes me breakfast.

I climbed out of my car and started up the stairs to my apartment. "Hi, Mike, how's it going?"

He paused his watering and looked up. "Just fine, baby girl. How's things with you?"

I exhaled a deep breath. "My probation car was stolen this afternoon, and the thief crashed it into a septic truck full of shit." I leaned against the handrail. "So, it's been a day I'll never be able to forget, for all the wrong reasons."

His eyebrows scrunched together. "Did they catch the thief?"

"Not yet, but we know who she is."

This time his eyebrows raised up into his forehead. "She?"

"Yeah, one of my probationers. It's not the first car she's stolen."

He shook his head and began watering again. "Well, I hope they catch her soon."

I started up the stairs. "Yeah, me too."

I walked into my apartment and smiled at Randolph, my pet goldfish. Randolph's been with me since I moved in three years ago. He's a trooper. He's stood by my side through thick and thin, and he never complains. All he asks is that I feed him twice a day, change the water once a week and keep the neighbor's cat from sneaking in and eating him. It's a match made in heaven.

"I'll get you some dinner as soon as I change," I said as I passed by his bowl on the kitchen counter.

I peeled off my work clothes and took a quick shower. After the day I'd had, I needed it. I pulled on a pair of gray sweatpants and a Fresno State T-shirt, grabbed the container of gourmet goldfish food and sprinkled a pinch into Randolph's glass bowl. I imagined he smiled his appreciation and waved at me with a tiny orange fin as he gobbled it up.

As I reached for the last SLO Pale Ale in the fridge, my stomach growled. I hoped Tate didn't forget the pizza.

The thought of pizza brought back memories of our first date, four years ago. It had taken me two hours to figure out what to wear. Sexy or casual? I'd wanted to knock her socks off but not look too eager. Casual? Should I try to look like I didn't really care what she thought? What if she took that as a sign I wasn't interested? I had to find a middle ground. I settled on skinny black jeans and a rust-colored, scoop-neck silk blouse that draped just enough to show a little cleavage.

I hadn't wanted to seem too eager, so I arrived ten minutes late. When I walked in, Tate was sitting on a stool, talking to a nice-looking, obviously gay young man behind the bar. As I approached, she turned to look at me, and a huge smile lit up her face. She stood and pulled out the stool beside her. She smelled like citrus. She introduced me to Ian, the bartender who took our order, a SLO Stout for her and a Pale Ale for me.

We moved to a small table in the corner of the room. Ian brought our drinks, set them on the table, winked, and returned to the bar.

Tate raised her glass. "Here's to making up for lost time."

I clinked my glass against hers. "And to the future."

"And to the future," she repeated, the grin on her face mischievous. "So, what have you been up to since you left for college? You didn't come back much."

How did she know I hadn't been back much? Had she kept tabs on me?

I raised an eyebrow. "Did you keep track of my comings and goings? That sounds a little stalkerish."

She laughed. "Your mom and my mom are friends, remember? They talk. And I see your sister at the gym."

So, she hadn't been keeping track of me. Her knowing about me was just a coincidence. Darn, I kinda liked the thought of her stalking me.

"Funny, my sister never said anything about talking to you." The gym would explain Tate's fabulous shoulders.

"We chat." She shrugged. "So, the last five years?"

It was my turn to shrug. "I finished high school and went to Fresno State, end of story."

She leaned her head to the side. "Nothing interesting happened in those five years? No boyfriends? Girlfriends? Come on, you must have broken a few hearts."

I took a deep breath and wiped at the condensation forming on my glass. "If you must know, I was the one who ended up with a broken heart." Tears threatened, and I fought to keep them where they belonged.

She placed her fingers under my chin and lifted my head. "I'm sorry, you don't have to talk about it if you don't want to."

"No, it's okay. It's been almost a year. You'd think I'd be over it." I wiped a tear away before it escaped down my cheek.

"Breakups are never easy." She handed me a napkin, and I wiped away another tear.

"No, they aren't." I wiped my nose. Not the sexiest thing to do on a date. "I'd come home early. Imagine my surprise when I walked in on her fucking her best friend."

Tate placed her hand on mine. "I'm so sorry."

"We'd been living together for almost a year. I planned to ask her to marry me that weekend."

"She didn't deserve you."

"No, she didn't." I took a sip of my beer. "Enough about my sordid past. What about you? Any skeletons in your closet?"

She chuckled and let go of my hand. "No, no skeletons. I've dated a few women, but nothing serious or long-term."

I leaned my head to the side and half-smiled. "What? I'd think you'd have women flocking to your door."

She laughed. "Did you forget while you were away in the big city that San Luis Obispo isn't exactly a hotbed of lesbian activity?"

I grinned. "No, but there are lesbians here. I'm sure you could have found one to settle down with."

She looked at me and raised an eyebrow. "Maybe I just haven't found the right lesbian yet."

"Touché." I paused. "Did you always know you wanted to be a cop?"

She shook her head. "No. Other than play basketball, I didn't know what I wanted. I knew I wanted to stay in SLO, but going to Cal Poly didn't interest me. My mom suggested I go to community college for a few years and figure it out."

"Did you play basketball?"

"I did, but the team wasn't all that good. But while I was there, I took a criminal justice class, and it clicked. I was fascinated. The system is so complex and dysfunctional. I ended up majoring in it and then went to the police academy. When I graduated, the PD here was hiring, and the rest is history." She picked up her glass and took a long swallow.

I loved the curve of her throat, and her neck begged to be kissed. I had to force myself to look away.

She looked at me and smiled. "How about you? Did you always want to be a probation officer?"

"No, and I don't plan on being one for long." I laughed. "I went to Fresno thinking I wanted to be a winemaker. I loved the idea of working on a vineyard and making juice into wine." I lifted my half-empty glass. "But I found that I liked the taste of a good ale better, and there wasn't a degree in beer making. Like you, I'd taken a criminology class and was hooked. One of my professors was a retired FBI agent, and he brought in several agents to talk to us. I was ready to sign up right then."

"You want to be an FBI agent?" Her forehead wrinkled into a question.

"Absolutely. I'll be twenty-three next year, so I can apply now."

Tate stared into her glass then she looked at me, I couldn't read her expression. "So, you don't plan on staying in SLO?"

I shook my head. "The academy is in Virginia, so I'd go there for at least six months. Then they could send me for more training or assign me to a field office." I picked up my glass and looked at her over the rim. "That could be anywhere in the country." I wasn't sure what she was thinking. Was she relieved I wouldn't be sticking around, avoiding any possibility of a serious commitment? Or was she disappointed something serious wasn't in our future?

She drained her beer and set the glass on the table. "Well, Riley Reynolds, it sounds like you've got your future all planned out."

Her tone sounded a little mocking, and I didn't like it. "Don't you? Aren't you planning on staying here and working at the PD for the next thirty years?"

Her jaw tightened, then relaxed. "Yes, I guess I do."

We sat looking at each other. I wondered if she'd want to see me again if there wasn't any future in it. "In any case, they won't be taking applications for another six months. And the hiring process can take a year. So, I'm not going anywhere anytime soon."

"So, in the meantime, we could hang out, have fun, and not worry about the future." It sounded like a statement, not a question.

I raised an eyebrow. "Are you interested in hanging out and having some fun?"

Her smile had been mischievous. "Oh, I'm interested, Riley Reynolds. I'm very interested."

A loud knock on the door drew me back to the present. I peered out the peephole, Tate stood there. I couldn't decide what was sexier, her in baggy faded blue jeans and a green sweatshirt or the pizza box and six-pack of beer she was holding. I opened the door and let my eyes trail from her feet to the smile on her face that said she had things on her mind other than pizza.

"I wasn't expecting you until later." I took the beer, handed her one, and put the rest in the fridge.

She set the pizza on my tiny kitchen table, unscrewed the top of the beer and took a long swallow. Damn. Watching her throat as she chugged the beer was hot.

"I needed to get your statement on the fire, and I thought I'd fill you in on your dead guy."

I could feel my eyebrows scrunch together. "*My* dead guy? He's *my* dead guy?"

"That's what Skylar and Cup are calling him."

"I don't find that very funny. Just cuz I found him doesn't make him mine. I don't even know who he is."

Tate pulled plates from the cabinet and forks from the drawer. "Then you're in luck because Skylar called me with an update."

I leaned against the counter and crossed one ankle over the other, enjoying watching Tate in my kitchen. "Why?"

She stopped what she was doing and looked at me. "Why what?"

"Why would Skylar update you on a homicide? You're in property crimes."

She shrugged and went back to putting napkins on the table. "She knows we're seeing each other. Hell, the whole department knows." She opened the pizza box and took out a slice. "She knew you'd be up all night wondering about it, so she filled me in."

She picked up another slice and plopped it on a plate. "The dead guy's name is Archie Abercrombie. Someone stabbed him in the back several times with a blade that must've been at least six inches long." She took a bite of pizza, then picked up the beer, and took a long swallow. I couldn't stop looking at her neck as she guzzled the beer. She had a gorgeous neck. "He ran a chop shop out of a warehouse in Paso Robles."

"So that's how Pinky knew him."

"That's the theory."

"I can't see Pinky killing him. She's never been violent that I know of."

Tate wiped her mouth with her napkin. "Well, as of now, thanks to your intel, she's the only suspect."

"What about the black BMW that drove by?"

"Sue said they'd check the area to see if there were any security cameras. Planned Parenthood next door probably has a few."

"Shit. I need to find her before they do." I stood, pulled two more beers from the refrigerator, and handed one to Tate.

"Riley, you need to let them do their job. It's a murder investigation now. Not just an auto theft." She unscrewed the top of the beer and pointed it at me.

I shook my head. "She's my probationer, and I have a warrant for her. I'm going to find her and bring her in." I stared at Tate, daring her to tell me not to go after Pinky, but she didn't. She knew that once I made my mind up, no one, not even a sexy blond friend with benefits, could change it.

"Okay. What about the fire? What did you see?" She took a small notebook from her back pocket and retrieved a pen from my collection on the counter.

"I was in the car waiting for Patty. A white guy with a shaved head ran out of the alley like the devil was chasing him. He ran up Higuera and almost knocked Patty over. Luckily, she didn't drop our drinks." I absentmindedly picked a slice of pepperoni off the pizza and popped it into my mouth. "When I looked back, there was smoke coming out of the alley."

"Other than white and shaved head, did you notice anything else about him?"

I closed my eyes and thought for a second. "It was hard to tell his age. Not young but not old either. He was big, close to six feet. Maybe two hundred pounds." I paused. "Faded blue jeans, grungy white T-shirt. And something on his left forearm. But I don't think it was a tattoo…a scar, maybe?"

"Had you seen him before?"

I pursed my lips and raised my eyes to the ceiling. "He seemed familiar, but I can't tell you why." I reached for another slice of pepperoni and Tate slapped my hand away.

"Stop picking at the pizza," she said. "Can you think of anything else?"

"Yeah. When he saw the probation car across the street I think it freaked him out."

"So maybe he's on probation?"

I shrugged. "Maybe." I drained the rest of my beer. "Are we done?"

She rolled her eyes. "I guess so."

"I recorded the Stanford women's game last night. Want to curl up on the couch and watch it?"

"Sure, that sounds like a perfect lesbian date night activity." Tate smiled at me lasciviously.

I stopped chewing and looked at her. "Date?" I said suspiciously. "This isn't a date, is it?"

Tate smiled and shook her head. "Relax, Riley. I'm not renting a U-Haul…Yet."

"Tate, the FBI—"

"Have you even applied?"

I looked away. Actually, I hadn't. "No. But I am as soon as they're recruiting again."

Tate let out an exasperated sigh. "Okay, Riley. Whatever you say. Let's go watch the game."

An hour later, the game was forgotten. Tate had my shirt off and my pants unzipped. I couldn't help but think about her handcuffs. I suggested we move to the bedroom. The bed was much more comfortable—and it had a headboard.

CHAPTER FIVE

When I woke up the next morning, Tate was gone, as usual. I dragged my butt out of bed, a little sore in a few places, but it would be a pleasant reminder of the things Tate had done to me and I to her. Even though I didn't want to make any commitments or have an official relationship, I couldn't deny our chemistry was off the charts.

After a quick shower, I dressed in my standard black polo and khaki pants. As I headed out, I said good morning to Randolph as he happily swam in circles around his little glass house.

On the way to the office, I stopped at The Black Horse Bakery and picked up two blueberry bagels with cream cheese and a cup of black coffee. A few minutes later, I walked into the office, said hi to a few people, then found Patty at her desk. I took a bagel out of the bag and handed it to her.

"Thanks. What's the occasion?"

I sat at my desk and took a bite of the still-warm bagel. "What? Can't I just be a thoughtful coworker and bring my pregnant officemate a bagel?"

She chuckled. "Sure, you can go with that. Or tell me what you've got up your sleeve."

Patty and I had been working together for over a year and she knew me well. I couldn't hide much from her.

I leaned back in my 1960s-era office chair and put my feet on the desk. "We need to find Pinky before the cops do. She's their main suspect. It might not end well if they find her, and she tries to run." I took a bite of the bagel and wiped my mouth with the back of my hand before I continued, "I'm sure she didn't kill that guy. I've known Pinky since she was sixteen. She's not a killer. A thief, yes. A killer, no way." My phone rang, but I let it go to voice mail and took another bite of the bagel.

"Do you think she's just going to let us arrest her without a fight?" Patty looked down at her bulging belly. "I'm not exactly in fighting condition." She massaged her abdomen with both hands.

"If she knows the cops are after her for murder, I think she'll let us take her in rather than risk getting shot." The light on my phone flashed. Whoever had called left a voice mail. I lifted the receiver, tapped in my code, and put it on speaker.

"Officer Reynolds, it's Pinky. I didn't kill Archie. He was my friend." Her normally squeaky voice took on an even higher pitch. "I was there, but when the BMW pulled up in front of the house, I knew it was time to bounce, and I took off out the back door." There was a short pause. "I know who killed Archie. Call me." She rattled off a number then the line went dead.

I looked at Patty. "Well shit, maybe she'll come to us."

I dialed the number, and Pinky answered on the first ring.

"Reynolds?"

"Yes. Where are you?"

She hesitated. I could hear traffic in the background, but it didn't give me a clue as to where she was.

"Pinky, you need to let me pick you up on the warrant. If the cops find you first, it won't be good. You're their only suspect right now."

"Riley, I didn't kill him, I swear." She was talking a mile a minute. "I was there. But I bounced when the Beamer pulled up."

"Pinky, who was in the BMW?"

"Lester Knight," she said, barely audible over the street noise.

"The gang leader?"

"Yeah, the freaking gang leader."

"Why did he kill Archie?"

"It's all my fault. I boosted a cherry Mustang from the university parking lot and delivered it to Archie's warehouse. He chopped it up for parts."

"The car belonged to Knight?"

"He'd bought it for his daughter. I swear I didn't know. I'd never have taken it if I had."

"Does he know you're the one who stole it?"

"I don't know. He might."

"Did he see you?"

"I don't think so. I took off out the back before he even got to the front."

"The house had been torn apart. Do you know what he was looking for?"

She hesitated. "Can't think of anything. Maybe to make it look like a burglary gone bad?"

That would make sense, I thought. I ran a hand through my hair. "Pinky, let me come get you."

Silence again. I could hear a big truck rumble by in the background.

"No. I'm leaving town. Somewhere no one will find me. Not even the cops." The line went dead.

I slammed the phone back on its cradle. "Shit!"

"Any ideas?" Patty asked.

"No." I grabbed my jacket off the back of the chair. "Let's go talk to her girlfriend. Maybe she knows something."

Twenty minutes later, we pulled up in front of the prep school across the street from the green house. It was surprisingly cute and well-maintained. Orange dahlias and pink mums filled the flower beds, and a lemon tree filled the air with the smell of citrus.

Pinky's girlfriend's name was Trixie Adams. In my head, I pictured a skinny, petite redhead in super femme clothes. Boy, was I wrong. At my knock, the door opened, and the biggest, butchest woman I'd ever seen stood before me.

"Who er you?" she asked without interest.

"Officer Reynolds," I said, showing her my ID. "This is Officer Painter." I motioned to Patty. "I'm Pinky's probation officer. Have you seen her?"

Trixie laughed. "If I had, do you think I'd tell you?"

"Can we come in and talk?"

"Hell no."

"Look, Trixie, Pinky's in a lot of trouble. A friend of hers was murdered—"

"Who?" Trixie's eyes grew wide.

"Archie Abercrombie. And the cops think she did it. And the real killer may be looking for her."

"Shit. That woman could not keep a low profile if her life depended on it. I love her to death, but she wears me out." She turned and walked away but left the door open. I looked at Patty. She shrugged. I guess we had the okay to enter the house.

The inside was neat and clean. The furniture looked secondhand but in good condition. The walls were painted a pale yellow and trimmed in white. A picture of Pinky and Trixie in Halloween costumes, Pinky dressed as Tinkerbell and Trixie as Captain Hook, sat on the fireplace mantle.

"Does Pinky live here?" I nodded to the picture of the two of them.

"No, not that I don't want her to. She's not ready to settle down."

Pinky and I had that in common. I wondered what her excuse was. "Any idea where she might be?"

"There's no telling. She has friends from the Canadian border to Mexico City. And you already know she has no problem acquiring transportation. She could be anywhere."

"When was the last time you talked to her?"

"She was here last night. She was gone before the sun came up."

Just like someone else I know. I pictured the other side of my bed empty this morning.

"Did she say anything about what happened yesterday?"

"Not a thing. I had no idea Archie was dead." Trixie sat on the faux leather couch and reached for a pack of Marlboros. "She never let on." She took out a cigarette and placed it between her lips. "That woman is going to be the death of me," she said as she lit the cigarette.

"Lester Knight may be looking for her. You might not be safe either."

Trixie blew out a lungful of smoke, leaned back on the couch, crossed an ankle over her knee, and smiled. "Don't you worry about me. I can protect myself." She winked.

I had no doubt she could.

I handed her my business card. "Call me if you hear from her?"

She chuckled. "Sure thing, officer," she said as she pocketed the card.

We left the house and walked across the street. Just as we got to the car, the black BMW with tinted windows came around the corner.

"Shit. Patty, get down." I ran to the other side of the car and knelt. I quickly took my cell phone out and started taking pictures. The car sped by, tires squealing around the corner.

"Okay, they're gone. You can get up."

I walked back to the driver's side and got in. Patty was slowly rubbing her belly. "Are you okay?"

"Yeah. I'm fine."

I opened the picture app on my phone and scrolled through a dozen pictures. "I'm going to call Tate real quick."

"What about the detectives assigned to the case?"

"I like Sue, but Cup's an asshole," I said, pulling Tate's number up on my phone.

After two rings, she answered. "Hey, babe, what's up? Please tell me it's not another dead body."

"Not funny, Tate."

"Okay, then, what's up? I only have a minute. There's been another fire on Higuera a few blocks further north."

"Crap. Which building?"

"The dumpster behind B of A."

"Shit, that's only a few blocks from my place. Is it the same guy?"

"Yeah. Two witnesses saw him running from the scene. I think they may have spooked him into dropping a gas can. We're hoping to get prints off it."

"Lucky break."

"Yeah. So, it's not that I don't love the sound of your voice, but I gotta go."

"Wait, Tate. The black BMW drove by Pinky's girlfriend's house as we were leaving. I got pictures, but I already know whose it is. Pinky called the office. She was at Archie's but took off when the Beamer pulled up."

"Who is it?" she asked, now interested.

"Lester Knight."

"Shit. That's not good."

"Pinky unknowingly stole a car that belonged to Knight's daughter, and Archie chopped it up."

"Did Knight see you?"

"He had to have seen the probation car. If he puts two and two together, he could figure out we're the same POs who were at Archie's house yesterday."

"All right, send me the pictures, and I'll pass them on to Cup and Skylar."

"I'm sending them now."

"Okay, I'll call you when I'm done at the scene."

I ended the call and looked at Patty. "There was another fire on Higuera. This time at the B of A." I started the car and pulled away from the curb.

"Looks like a pattern," Patty said.

"Yeah, and I don't like that it's just a few blocks from my apartment." I merged onto Monterey Street and headed back to the office. "They might be able to get a print off the gas can he dropped."

"Let's hope Tate IDs him before anyone gets hurt."

We headed back to the office as there were plenty of other wayward probationers to find besides Pinky, a truth reinforced by a stack of files on my chair. Stan must have dropped them there. I looked over at Patty's desk. No new files. I looked at her.

She raised a shoulder. "He likes me better than you."

I glared at her, knowing it was probably true.

I hadn't heard back from Tate by five, so I stopped at the mini-mart a block from my apartment and picked up a six-pack of pale ale and a quart of coffee-chocolate chip ice cream for dinner.

Once home, I put the ice cream in the freezer and the beer in the fridge, locked my gun in the safe and sprinkled fish food in Randolph's bowl, and told him about my day. He was more interested in the orange and red flakes floating in the water.

The light on the answering machine was flashing red. I pushed the button. The first one was my mother. She didn't like to bother me at work, so she always called my house phone rather than my cell phone. She reminded me to invite Tate to Sunday dinner, for the hundredth time. My family hadn't given up hope that Tate and I would settle into wedded bliss and have babies. I shook my head. That wasn't likely to happen anytime soon, if ever.

After the beep, the second message began to play. At first, it was just heavy breathing, and I almost laughed at the thought of someone leaving me an obscene message. But then, a deep, menacing voice began. "Do you like the fires, bitch? I'm getting closer."

My heart pounded in my chest, and the fight or flight response took hold. My first thought was to grab Randolph and get out of there. I picked up his glass bowl and held it against my chest. He wasn't worried in the least, he continued to swim in circles, oblivious to the threat.

I set the bowl back on the counter, pulled out my cell phone, and called Tate. I hated feeling helpless. I had a gun, and I'd been trained to use it. I'd never had to shoot anyone, but I think I could if I had to.

I walked to the front door and made sure it was locked. After two rings, Tate answered. "Hi, babe," she said, sounding like she didn't have a care in the world.

I checked the window and pulled the living room blinds closed. "Tate, have you caught the arsonist?" I could hear my voice. I didn't like being scared. I didn't even watch scary movies. The last thing I needed was my very own horror show.

"Riley wha—"

"He called."

"Who called?"

"The arsonist, he left a message on my answering machine."

"At work or home?"

"Home. Tate, how did he get my home phone number?"

"I don't know, Riles. What did he say?"

I paced back and forth across my tiny living room, four steps to the wall and four steps back to the door. "He asked if I liked the fires, then said he was getting close."

"Shit."

I walked into the bedroom and checked to make sure the windows were locked.

"Double-check the door and windows. I'm on my way," she said before she hung up.

I walked back into the kitchen, sat at the table, and looked at Randolph swimming aimlessly around in his tiny home without a care in the world. I'd been like that only thirty minutes ago, minus the water and the clear glass bowl. Thirty minutes ago, the most concerning thing on my mind was finding Pinky and figuring out my relationship with Tate. Now, I had to worry about a madman who liked fire and seemed to hate me for some unknown reason.

I pulled a beer from the refrigerator, dropped back into the chair and took a long swallow. Was the arsonist on probation? Or maybe a former probationer? Maybe someone I'd sent to prison? In my four years as a probation officer, I'd had my share of crazy clients. Gerald, the guy who suffered from schizophrenia and saw ninjas came to mind. The ninjas were his guardians. They weren't very good at their job since they were the reason he'd ended up in jail and on probation. He'd led the police on a high-speed chase through the county. The ninjas had told him the cops were out to kill him, so when a cop tried to pull him over for going the wrong way on a one-way street, he panicked and began driving like a bat out of hell, the ninjas yelling at him the whole time that the police were going to kill him. He crashed into a fence on a back road in Templeton. Then he fought with the cops, yelling, "Don't kill me! Don't kill me! Don't kill me!" at the top of his lungs.

But I'd never had someone who wanted to kill me. At least no one had ever threatened me to my face. By the time Tate arrived, I'd finished the beer and opened another.

"Starting tomorrow, we'll review all your old probation files," she said.

"All of them?"

"I guess we could eliminate the females and men over forty."

"And anyone not white, but I suppose he could have been a light-skinned Latinx."

"So, we're looking for a male, between the ages of eighteen and forty, white or light-skinned Latinx, maybe a scar on his forearm. And he may have been on probation and on your caseload."

I nodded.

"I'll have the tech guys search probation databases for those characteristics and see if we can narrow it down." She opened the refrigerator. "Do you have anything to eat?"

"There's cheese. And probably some crackers in the cabinet. I haven't been to the store in a while."

I watched as Tate took a package of Irish cheddar from the fridge and a box of saltines from the cabinet. She looked at home in my kitchen, almost too at home. Should I be worried?

"You know you could take some time off. Go somewhere? Maybe take your Aunt Liz to Vegas?"

"First of all, I'm not going to let this guy scare me into leaving town." I took a deep breath. "And I don't want to contribute to my aunt's gambling issues." I paused. "Oh, and my mother wants me to invite you to dinner on Sunday." I picked up a takeout menu off the table and began reading it.

Tate arranged cheese on the saltines, then transferred them to a paper plate, placed it on the table, and sat across from me.

"So, your mother invited me to dinner?" She picked up a cracker and cheese and popped it into her mouth.

I didn't look up from the menu. "Yes, she did."

"What about you?"

"What about me?"

"Do you want me to come to dinner at your parents' house?"

I turned the menu over and looked at the back. "If you want to. You know my sister will be there, and what a pain she can be. And my nephew. He's a holy terror."

"All three-year-olds are holy terrors." She popped another cracker-and-cheese bite into her mouth.

"And then Aunt Liz will tell you all about how Uncle Lou is screwing his bimbo in her house. Or she'll have won at the casino and want to tell you every detail, or she lost a ton of money, and the dealers are all thieves and cheats." I gauged her reaction. She was smiling. Damn.

"Riley, if you don't want me to go, just say so. You don't have to make up stories about how horrible your family is to scare me away."

I continued to peruse the menu. "I'm not trying to scare you away. Just warning you that it won't be a nice quiet dinner. Although my mom is a fantastic cook, and Aunt Liz makes great pie. You'll have to put up with a lot of craziness in exchange."

"I'm a cop. I can handle crazy."

I could feel Tate watching me, but I didn't look up.

"Do you want to order Chinese?" she asked.

"Sure."

"Then why are you staring at the menu for the Italian place like you're going to die if you don't have Italian food in the next ten minutes?"

She caught me. I hadn't read anything on the menu. "Shut up."

I threw the menu at her. She grabbed my wrist and pulled me across the table until our faces were only inches apart. I could feel her breath on my cheek. One corner of her lips curled into a smile, and she whispered, "Or, we could skip dinner and eat other things?" Her blue eyes sparkled like diamonds. My heart raced. I was sure she could hear it. I tried to be cool, to not let her know how turned on I was.

I pulled back an inch and said, "I need a shower." I slid off the table, pulled my T-shirt over my head, and walked into my bedroom, hoping she'd follow. I didn't have to wait long.

When the hot water ran out, I turned the handle off and reached for a towel. Tate, however, had other ideas. She wrapped her arms around my waist, lifted me off my feet, and took me to the bed. She pushed me onto my back, her blue eyes focused on my mouth the whole time. She stuck her index finger in her mouth and sucked on it, then slowly pulled it out, placed the wet tip of her finger just below my bare anklebone and slowly drew a circle around it, a trail of saliva glistened in the light.

She stuck her finger back in her mouth and slowly drew it out halfway, then slid it back in and out, all the way this time. She returned her finger to the place just above my ankle where she'd left off and slowly ran it up the side of my lower leg to the sensitive spot behind my knee. She returned her digit to her mouth, lubricating it again before returning it to the spot just above the back of my knee and slowly continued her sojourn up the back of my leg. When she reached where my leg met my butt, she replaced her finger with her tongue and continued up my cheek, straddled my thighs, her wetness resting on my legs. It was exquisite torture.

She placed her hands on either side of my shoulders, leaned down, and kissed from the base of my back to my neck. Chills raced up my spine, the wetness between my legs dripping onto the sheets. Her tongue moved to my ear, and her breath was hot against my skin. I must have whined. The game she played with my body was delicious agony. I needed her to touch me. I needed her inside me.

"Tate, please," I begged, trying to turn over.

She pinned my hands on either side of my head and lay flat against me, pushing her wetness against my ass. "Too bad I don't have handcuffs with me," she whispered, making me shiver.

My breath hitched at the thought of her restraining me, making me her captive. "God, Tate, please. I need you inside." I raised my hips up, wanting her in me.

"Shhhhh," she whispered. "All in good time." She let go of my hands, slid a hand down my ass, and entered me from behind with two fingers. She allowed me to rise to my knees, her other hand holding tight to my shoulder, using the leverage to slowly plunge into me again and again.

I rocked back against her, wanting more. Wanting all of her inside me. "More," I begged. "Tate, please..." She slid a third finger in and drove deeper inside me, the fingers of her other hand digging into my shoulder. I knew I'd have bruises, but I didn't care as she rode me hard, and I bucked again and again. I felt like I was on fire, so close to exploding. "Don't stop," I cried. "Don't stop. God, don't stop."

"Come for me, Riley, come for me," she said, rocking hard against my ass, pushing her fingers deeper.

"Yes, Tate, yes—" My brain exploded in a kaleidoscope of colors and energy so intense I felt like I'd been struck by lightning, and wave after wave of pleasure rolled through my body, gradually slowing until I collapsed back on the bed, exhausted.

She lay on top of me, her heartbeat racing against my bare back. "God, Riley, you're amazing," she breathed in my ear. "I lo—"

I jerked up, and she rolled off. "Don't say it. Don't ruin it by going there." I swung my legs over the side of the bed.

Tate slapped the mattress with her hand. "Come on, Riley, you know I lo—"

"Don't say it, Tate." I stood, taking the sheet with me, leaving her naked, her muscled abs glistening with sweat. "I need another shower," I said, fighting the pull to climb back into bed. "You're welcome to join me, but no talking." I dropped the sheet and walked naked into the bathroom. Before I could close the door, she was behind me, wrapping her arms around my waist.

"Someday, you'll give in," she whispered as she pinched my nipple between two fingers, sending sparks to my center.

"Maybe. But right now, you need to fuck me again." I turned in her arms and wrapped my legs around her waist.

CHAPTER SIX

The next morning, I gingerly walked into my office with a smile on my face and carefully sat down at my desk. Certain parts of my body were tender, but I enjoyed the reminder of my night with Tate. It wasn't often that she spent the entire night and was still in my bed when I woke up. We'd continued the previous night's activities in the shower this morning. My knees were a little sore from kneeling on the tile as I made Tate come with my mouth. I sat at my desk and remembered how her breathing had grown more erratic as she got closer and closer. Her hands tangled in my hair, pushing me harder into her center. Then her hips began to shake, and she cried out as she came. When it ended, she melted on the shower floor next to me, letting her breathing return to normal. We held each other until the water turned cold.

The message light on my phone was blinking, so I lifted the receiver and tapped in the code.

"Officer Reynolds, this is Lena Higgins, Pinky's mother. I went through some things Pinky left here and found a name and address where she might be. His name's Freddy. I don't know the last name, but the address is 2700 Victoria Avenue. She called last night to let me know she was okay but wouldn't tell me where she was. I'm really worried. Please let me know if you find her."

I jotted down the information and went looking for Stan. I found him in the break room, biting into a glazed jelly donut. Red raspberry jelly clung to his chin—or he'd cut himself shaving and it was blood.

"Good morning, Stan," I said as he took another bite of the donut, then wiped his chin with the back of his hand. Jelly, not blood.

"Morning," he said with his mouth full. "Your car is ready. You can pick it up at the county yard."

"Any news about the investigation? I swear it was locked."

"Inconclusive. There's no way to know for sure if it was locked or unlocked." He scowled. "And since the woman who stole it is a known car thief, the chief's giving you the benefit of the doubt."

I smiled. "Good."

"Anything else, or can I finish my donut?"

"Oh, yeah, I have an address where Pinky might be hiding. As soon as Patty gets here, we'll head over there." I started to walk away, and he stopped me.

"Reynolds."

I turned back to look at him. "Yes?"

"You better make sure you cross all your T's and dot all your I's. The chief won't be so forgiving if you screw up again."

I opened my mouth to say that I hadn't screwed up but decided it wasn't the hill to die on. I walked back to my office, grinding my teeth, wanting to punch something.

Patty was sitting at her desk with a cup of tea when I walked back into our office. "Good morning," she said as bright and cheery as a daisy.

"You're eight months pregnant. Why are you so cheery this morning?"

She grinned from ear to ear. "Today's my last day. I start maternity leave on Monday."

"Great." The thought didn't make me happy. I'd have to work with someone I'd probably like a lot less for the six months she'd be off. "Since you're here today, I need you to take a ride with me. Pinky's mother called with an address where she might be."

"I'd be happy to, as long as no dead bodies are involved."

"Hilarious." I flipped her the bird. "Stan said my car is ready, so you can drop me off at the county yard after we check it out." I slipped my arm in the sleeve of my probation jacket.

"I hope they got the smell out," she said, trying not to laugh.

Twenty minutes later, we pulled up in front of a run-down, gray, single story, Craftsman house. Two of the three steps up to the faded red front door were broken, and we had to be careful where we placed our feet. I knocked. I could hear movement inside, but no one came to the door. I tried to look in the window but couldn't see anything between the spiderweb of cracks and a layer of dirt. I knocked again. "Probation Department, please open the door." I really didn't have any authority. As far as I knew, this Freddy person wasn't on probation, although he might be since he was a friend of Pinky's.

"I'm going to go around the back of the house and look around. You wait here, okay?"

Patty nodded as she carefully walked down the steps to stand a few feet away from the door in case anyone tried to run out. More for self-preservation than to stop someone from fleeing.

As I rounded the corner, a short, pudgy, bald guy in purple and pink boxers smacked into me and landed on his butt. Before he could right himself, I grabbed him by the arm and pulled him to his feet. I knew this guy. "Manny?"

Manny Martinez was a well-known burglar. His only saving grace was that he only broke into businesses, not people's homes. I also knew there was a warrant for him for failing to report to his probation officer, who was me. And he'd been AWOL for a year and a half.

"Officer Reynolds, what are you doing here?" His eyes darted around the yard.

"Me? What are you doing here? Last I heard, you were hiding out in Mexico."

"I came back for my mother's birthday." He smiled. "She's eighty." I knew his fingers were crossed behind his back.

"Where's Freddy?"

"Not here. He's at his old lady's place."

"What's Freddy's last name?"

"Murphy," Manny said.

"Freddy Murphy, the loan shark?"

He shrugged. "Loan shark, bookie. He's got a hand in a lotta things. I guess you could call him an entrepreneur."

Yeah, I thought, an entrepreneur of criminal enterprises. "What's his girlfriend's name?"

"Mindy."

I exhaled and rolled my eyes. "Mindy what?"

"Carr. Like the football player."

"I don't watch football."

He looked at me like I had a second head.

"Where's she live?" I asked, my patience wearing thin.

His eyes darted to the gate that led to the front of the house, a sure sign he was getting ready to bolt.

"Uh, I don't know." He glanced at the gate again.

"Manny." I snapped my fingers in front of his face. He looked at me, but his right foot began tapping the ground. "I'm looking for Pinky Higgins. Have you seen her?"

He shook his head. "Not in a few weeks. Why you lookin' for her?"

"The cops want to talk to her, and she stole my car."

"She stole a probation car?" He laughed out loud. "She's one gutsy broad."

"Yeah, real gutsy."

"Did you try Archie's? She hangs out there a lot."

"He's dead, and she was the last person to see him alive."

The color drained from his face. "Archie's dead?"

"Yep, dead. I found him three days ago. He'd been stabbed in the back." I paused. "He really pissed off the wrong people this time."

Manny opened his mouth and without a word bolted like a jackrabbit on steroids. As he passed me I stuck out my foot, catching his lower leg, sending him headfirst into the side of the house. He melted to the ground. Just like in an episode of *The Three Stooges.*

Patty came waddling from the front of the house and looked at Manny lying on the ground. "Who the hell is that? And what did you do to him?"

"Manny Martinez. He was on my caseload two years ago. There's at least two warrants out for him." I shrugged. "He tried to run and tripped over my foot."

"He's out cold. Sorry, but I can't help you get him in the car." She rubbed her belly and smiled. She wasn't sorry at all.

I pulled my phone out and called Tate, knowing she'd be on duty. "What did you do now?" she asked without bothering to say hi.

"Why do you always assume I've done something wrong?"

"Because you always call me when you need help cleaning up a mess." I could tell she was trying not to laugh. "What's it this time?"

"I caught Manny Martinez."

"No shit?"

"No shit."

"I thought he was in Mexico."

"Well obviously he came back," I huffed. "I need help getting him into the back of my car."

"Did you shoot him?"

"No, of course not." I stood up straight and squared my shoulders.

"Okay, why can't you get him into your car?"

"He tried to make a run for it, and he tripped over my foot and crashed headfirst into a wall. He's out cold."

"He could have a concussion. Maybe you should call for an ambulance."

"And listen to Stan bitch about the department having to pay for it? No thanks, I'll drive him to the hospital myself."

"All right, text me the address and I'll be there in a few. And don't forget to handcuff him before he wakes up."

"Come on, I only forgot to do that once." I pulled out my handcuffs and attached a bracelet to each of Manny's wrists.

"Okay, I'm on my way." She chuckled before she hung up.

The jail was backed up with bookings, and we didn't get out of there until after five. I'd only been home a few minutes and was feeding Randolph when there was a knock at the front door. To be safe, I glanced out the window, you can never be too careful. Not that a psycho killer would knock before setting fire to my apartment, but you never know. Fortunately, Tate stood there with a pizza box, a six-pack of beer, and a frown on her face. Well, like the Meatloaf song said, two out of three ain't bad.

"What's wrong?" I asked as soon as I opened the door.

She walked in and set the pizza box on the counter. I could smell the pepperoni across the room and my stomach growled. She pulled two beers from the cardboard carrier and handed me one.

"Good news or bad news first?"

I narrowed my eyes and leaned my head to the side. "You know I hate when you lead with that. How about, 'Hi, honey, how was your day?'"

She took a long swallow of beer. "I never call you honey. Babe, maybe, but never honey. You're not the honey type." She took another sip. "How was your day?"

"Thanks for asking. No one stole my car or set fire to the dumpster out back, so I'd say it was pretty good."

Tate laughed as she took plates from the cabinet and opened the pizza box. The aroma of spicy grease and cheese made me drool. She lifted a slice, dropped it on a plate, and handed it to me.

"The good news is we figured out who the arsonist is."

I took a bite of my slice. It was still warm, and the cheese was still gooey. "Okay, and the bad news?"

She reached for the roll of paper towels on the counter, tore one off, and handed it to me. "Wellllll...There's bad news, and there's bad, bad news."

"Geez, Tate. What is it with you and bad, bad news?"

She shrugged. "I'm just the messenger."

I set my plate on the counter and folded my arms. "Okay, hit me with it."

"It's Max Maynard."

I scrunched my eyebrows and frowned. "But he's in prison. I sent him there three years ago."

"And he's out on parole as of a month ago."

I pulled a chair out from the tiny kitchen table and sat down. "At sentencing, he swore he'd come for me when he got out."

"And now he's out, and it looks like he's making good on his threat."

I rested my elbows on the table and lowered my head onto my palms. "Do you remember him from high school? He was in your grade."

"Yeah, he was odd, even back then."

"He was placed in foster care when he was five. His family's apartment was destroyed in a fire. His older brother died, and Max suffered third-degree burns on his arms and legs. His parents checked out and never regained custody of him."

Tate grabbed two more beers from the refrigerator and handed me one. "That's tragic."

"And to make it worse, one of his foster parents physically abused him. He probably still has the scars from that too."

"Jesus," Tate muttered. "I assume he or his brother set the fire at the apartment?"

"That was the theory, but they never determined which one."

"Can you pull his file? Maybe we can figure out where he's hiding."

"Who's his parole agent?" I asked, dreading the answer. I glared at her, daring her to tell me.

"You won't like it."

"It's Jack McCarthy. Isn't it?"

Tate pursed her lips and nodded.

Jack McCarthy was a misogynistic asshole who hated that women had ever been allowed to wear a badge. As far as he was concerned, the only time a woman needed handcuffs was in the bedroom. The thought of him sent the feeling of tiny ants crawling up my spine.

"He doesn't know where Max is?"

Tate shook her head. "He was at the Homestead Motel the week after he was released. He left and didn't notify McCarthy where he was going." She finished off the slice and wiped her hands on a paper towel. "What else do you remember about him?"

I took a long breath and looked at the unfinished slice of pizza, growing cold and losing its appeal. "When he was ten, he killed the neighbor's cat. They moved him to another foster home. The new foster parents noticed the bruises and called his social worker."

"Sexual?"

"He denied he'd been sexually abused, but he killed an animal, so it's certainly a possibility." I guzzled down half of the second beer. "And he did sexually assault a woman."

"That's why he was on probation?"

I nodded. "Then I caught him in possession of a firearm twice, so the judge sent him to prison."

"And he blames you."

"It doesn't make sense, but yeah, he does."

Tate grabbed another slice of pizza and then pulled a photo from her back pocket. "His parole agent gave me a copy of his release photo." She handed it to me.

I stared at the picture. A man with a shaved head and square jaw stared back at me. His eyes were as black as coal, and his nose looked like it had been broken more than once. I knew Max Maynard was the same age as Tate, but the man in the photo looked twice that. "Wow, this is not the guy I remember."

"Yeah, prison will do that to ya."

I continued to stare at the photo. This guy didn't look anything like the guy I'd asked a judge to send to prison three years ago, and nothing like the skinny, awkward kid he'd been in high school. What had prison done to him?

Tate nudged my arm. "Riley, did you hear what I said?"

I blinked to clear my head. "What?"

"I want to ask my lieutenant to have a car parked outside your apartment until we catch him."

I frowned. "No. Absolutely not. I'm a probation officer. I have a gun, and I've had plenty of training on how to use it."

Tate took my hand and squeezed. "Riley, the detail is just preventative. Hopefully, if he comes here and sees the car, he'll think twice about trying anything. It shouldn't be for too long. We know who he is. Now we just have to find him, and SLO isn't that big of a place."

I let go of her hand and crossed my arms. "No."

"What about a detail on your parents' house? Just in case."

I thought about how my parents would react. My dad wouldn't like it, but I did want them to be safe. "Okay. But you know my dad won't like it."

"I know. But he'll agree to it to keep your mom and sister safe. I'll call the lieutenant and get a car assigned ASAP." She punched in the number and put the phone to her ear.

I took my cold, limp pizza and beer into the living room and turned the television on. A few minutes later, Tate joined me.

"It's all set. He's sending one of the reserve officers."

I rested my head on her shoulder. "Thanks, Tate."

"Just doin' my job." She put her arm around me and kissed the top of my head.

An hour later, my phone chirped, and I looked at the screen. "It's my parents." I looked at Tate. "Do you want to explain it to them?"

Tate raised her hands like she was surrendering. "Oh, hell no."

I glared at her and answered the phone. "Hello," I said in the most laid-back voice I could conjure up, given the circumstances.

"Riley." My father's voice was just on this side of a yell.

I grimaced. "Hi, Dad, what's up?"

"Why is there a cop car parked in front of our house? What kind of trouble are you in?" he barked.

After my father had a heart attack two years ago, his doctor advised him to exercise and not let things upset him so much. My mother talked him into taking yoga classes and learning to meditate. Now the house could be on fire, and he'd be calm, cool, and collected. So, for him to raise his voice because a cop car was parked in front of the house had to mean he was really worried. Couldn't say that I blame him, a lunatic out to kill me was a worrisome situation.

"Dad, it's nothing to worry about. Tate thought it was a good idea, just to be safe." I was trying for nonchalance.

"Just to be safe from what, Riley?"

I looked at Tate for help, but she was peeling the label off her beer and refused to look up. "Well, Dad, there's this guy who just got out of prison, and it seems he's a little miffed at me."

"Miffed how?"

"Really, Dad, it's—"

"Riley, cut the BS. What's going on?"

I guzzled down the rest of my beer for courage. "He violated his probation three years ago. I arrested him and the judge sent him to prison based on my recommendation. So he blames me."

"That's ridiculous."

I wanted to laugh. "Yes, Dad, it is. But he's not the brightest bulb in the box, and he wants revenge."

"Revenge? How?"

"Dad, really—"

"Riley, I asked you a question."

"Okay, okay. He's been setting fires in dumpsters downtown."

"And…"

"And they're getting closer and closer to my apartment."

There was silence on the other end. I counted to ten, but still nothing from him. "Dad? You still there?"

"Yes," he said. "I don't like the idea of some thug wanting to hurt you."

Yeah, neither did I.

CHAPTER SEVEN

I usually spent Saturday mornings catching up on personal email and social media. I wasn't much for posting my business for the universe to see. In fact, I used a fake name on all my social media accounts. Only my friends knew that my username was QueerInSLO, and like I said, I mainly stalked others on Facebook and Instagram. I didn't want to have an extensive digital footprint. Being a probation officer, like being a cop, meant you kept a low profile. I had a post office box for my mail, and my voter registration and DMV information were confidential. As much as I could, I stayed off the radar and tried to keep my personal life from becoming too public.

But it wouldn't have surprised me if Max Maynard knew where I lived. We'd gone to school together since first grade. His family lived in the same neighborhood as mine until the fire, and he went into the foster care system. San Luis Obispo wasn't a huge town, so it would be pretty easy to find someone, especially if you'd lived here all your life.

The rest of the day, I planned on getting laundry done, curling up on the couch, and reading the latest Kat Jackson antiromance novel, *The Roads Left Behind Us*. I call it antiromance because she loves to flip romance tropes on their ear. Then I was going to make a pot of gooey mac and cheese. With real Irish cheddar, of course.

As I got up from the kitchen table to sort laundry, there was a knock on the front door. I wasn't expecting anyone, so my heart started to race, dreading that Max Maynard might be on the other side. I quietly approached and looked out the peephole. Tate stood there smiling at me from the other side, her blond hair styled to look messy.

I opened the door, and my eyebrows knit together. "What's going on?"

"Not even a good morning?"

"Good morning. Why are you here?" I still hadn't asked her in.

"Can I come in?"

I waited for a second, looking at her from head to toe. She looked good enough to eat in the black and white T-shirt, black board shorts, and flip-flops.

"Sure." I opened the door all the way. "What has you here so early on a Saturday morning?"

She grinned. "It's a perfect day to spend at the beach. I have a picnic basket, sunscreen, and an ice chest in the car. All you have to do is change into beach clothes. I have plenty of sunscreen."

I rolled my eyes and looked at the ceiling as I breathed. How arrogant of her to assume I would drop everything and go to the beach with her. But she did look really hot in board shorts, and it was a perfect day for the beach. What the hell? The laundry could wait, and I could read my book on the beach.

"So, you think you can waltz in here and expect me to drop everything at a moment's notice and go to the beach with you?" I wasn't going to make it easy for her.

Her eyes narrowed slightly, and she pursed her lips. "Sorry, I guess I should have called. I was so excited to have a day off and wake up to such a beautiful morning." She shoved her hands into the pockets of her board shorts and said quietly, "I wanted to spend it with you." The look on her face was so sincere it would have melted even Scrooge's heart.

If I hadn't already decided to go with her, I certainly would have now. "Okay, I'll go."

Forty-five minutes later, we pulled into the gravel parking lot at Montana de Oro State Beach, a small beach hidden between two large cliffs. To get there, you drive several miles down a narrow winding road south of Los Osos.

It was a warm, cloudless autumn day. Surprisingly, only a handful of people were there, sunning themselves and splashing in the water. No one was at the beach's south end, so we kicked off our flip-flops, grabbed our stuff, and headed in that direction, letting the grainy sand massage our feet.

When we got a good fifty feet from the other beachgoers, Tate laid out an old quilt, placed two sand chairs on top of it, then faced the water and pulled her T-shirt over her head. I couldn't help but stare at her perfect breasts nestled in a low-cut sports bra. Her muscled shoulders, arms, and abs begged to be touched.

I felt a nudge and pulled my gaze to her face.

"Riley, did you hear me?"

"What?" I stammered.

She held out a tube of sunscreen. "Will you rub some on my back?"

Would I rub some on her back? Seriously? I'd rub it all over her body if we weren't on a public beach. "Sure." I held my hand out, acting as unfazed as possible.

She handed me the tube and sat on the quilt, her back to me. The muscles across her back were just as impressive as the ones in front. I'd seen Tate naked more times than I could count, and she took my breath away every time. I never got tired of it.

I squeezed out a dollop of lotion and began applying it to her back, slowly massaging it in, getting every nook and cranny. Her head fell forward, and she moaned. I was instantly wet. Good thing I had a bathing suit on.

"That feels so good," she said. "If we weren't in public…"

"Whoa, tiger. Put that thought on hold." I laughed and handed the tube of sunscreen over her shoulder. "My turn." I pulled my T-shirt off. Tate's eyes roamed over my electric blue bathing suit, and she smiled.

"You don't make it easy on a girl," she said as I turned around, and she began rubbing lotion on my back. She was right. It did feel good, like never wanting her to stop "good."

"Okay, thanks." I moved away and bent to look in the ice chest. I pointed to the plastic pitcher containing a peachy, orange-colored liquid. "What's that?"

One side of Tate's mouth raised in a mischievous grin. "Sex on the Beach."

I slanted an eyebrow up. "Excuse me?"

"It's a drink. Haven't you ever had one?"

I shook my head. It was barely noon, and I wasn't sure that alcohol this early in the day was a good idea, especially on a public beach with Tate Walker.

She took two plastic cups out of the picnic basket. "Well, it's time to lose your virginity."

I couldn't help but laugh. "I guess it's five o'clock somewhere."

I leaned back in my sand chair, closed my eyes, and sipped Tate's sweet concoction. The gentle breeze carried a hint of salt and the smell of seaweed. The lapping of the waves against the shore created a hypnotic rhythm that almost put me to sleep.

"You look relaxed," Tate said just in time to keep me from dozing off.

I opened my eyes as a flock of pelicans flew over us. "I am." I turned to look at her. "Thank you. I didn't know how much I needed this."

She winked at me. "I think we both needed a break from the insanity."

I held out my cup. "Here's to less insanity."

She clinked her plastic cup against mine. "To less insanity," she repeated as she leaned over and kissed me.

The rest of the afternoon sped by. We splashed around in the frigid water, read, and relaxed in the sun. At four o'clock, having had plenty of time for our "Sex on the Beach" drinks to wear off, we packed up and headed back to SLO. Relaxed and satisfied.

I pulled into my parents' driveway at five o'clock on Sunday. Dinner wasn't until six, but I got there early so I could talk with Aunt Liz. Five years ago while I was away at college, Aunt Liz discovered that my Uncle Lou had a girlfriend on the side, so she left him. She ended up moving into my bedroom in my parents' house. Being Catholic, Aunt Liz believed divorce was a sin. So, she was still living in my room and still married to Uncle Lou, which was okay with him because he didn't have to pay alimony. He was still in the big house in Arroyo Grande doing his thing.

When I graduated from college, I moved back in with my parents. I told myself it was only temporary. Lucky for me, my father had turned the garage into a man cave while I was away at college. It had a fold-out sofa, a small refrigerator, and a big-screen TV. It didn't have its own bathroom, but otherwise, it had everything I needed and its own exterior door, so I could come and go as I pleased. My father wasn't happy about me taking over his space, but my mother wasn't giving up her sewing room and told Dad he could watch TV in the living room like everyone else. Dad stewed for weeks, but he didn't win that battle.

Today I needed to talk to Aunt Liz about the high-stakes underground poker room on Higuera Street. Unbeknownst to my father—her brother—my aunt was a regular participant. How my aunt wormed her way in is a mystery to me. From what I hear, she's very lucky and rarely leaves with less than she walked in with. I knew about the game in the back room of McGee's Irish Pub because I was friends with Sally Handley, a deputy prosecutor in the district attorney's office who occasionally sat in. According to Sally, the game was by invitation only.

As I walked to the front door, I waved to the officer sitting in a patrol car in front of my parents' house, and he waved back.

As the name suggested, my parents' neighborhood, known as "Old SLO," is in the older part of town, a few blocks from the public high school. Go Tigers! The houses weren't fancy, just the run-of-the-mill three-bedroom, two-bath Craftsmen, painted in standard tans, yellows, greens, and whites. The front lawns were traditionally maintained by fathers and sons, and flowerbeds by mothers and daughters. No one hired a gardener in our neighborhood. Why would you pay someone to do that when you could do it yourself?

The city of San Luis Obispo had an eclectic mix of residents. It boasted one of the best universities in the country, and thousands of students arrived every September and vanished every June. Because of the university, SLO had its fair share of wealthy families. Neither Tate's nor my family could be considered wealthy. My parents clung to our middle-class status by the skin of their teeth. There weren't any doctors, lawyers, or professors in our neighborhood. Most of the adults worked at one of the two hospitals in town or were motel or restaurant managers, mechanics, and teachers. Some were cops or firefighters.

When I walked in the front door, the aroma of something sweet baking in the oven filled the air. My Aunt Liz was a first-class baker. Years ago, she'd owned a pie shop in Grover Beach. It did well, and people came from all over the coast to buy her pies, especially for holidays. But that was before she'd had kids. Once she and Uncle Lou started a family, she closed the shop to be a stay-at-home mom. So now we were the lucky beneficiaries of her pie-making skills.

My father sat on the couch in the living room, watching a baseball game. My dad managed the local paint store, and my mother was a nurse. She worked in the emergency room at the county-run hospital, not the fancy Catholic one across town. She has a college education and makes more money than him. It's a sore spot, so we avoid the subject.

Today's game was the LA Dodgers and the New York Mets. Dad's a dyed-in-the-wool Dodger fan. I'm sure if he were ever injured, he'd bleed Dodger blue.

I leaned over the arm of the couch and gave him a hug. "Hi, Dad."

"Hi, Riley," he said, not looking away from the television. "How's your weekend?"

"Good." I continued into the kitchen, knowing he didn't really want to talk until the game was over.

My mother was standing at the kitchen sink washing a pan, my sister next to her with a towel, ready to dry. A few years ago, Angie had moved into an apartment with her boyfriend. We were Irish Catholics, and my dad disapproved of his daughter living in sin. My mother showed her disapproval by converting my sister's room into a sewing room. Three years ago, Angie found out she had a bun in the oven and the boyfriend announced he wasn't interested in being a baby daddy, so she moved back in with my parents. She and her now three-year-old son, Jamie, still live under my parents' roof.

I sat at the kitchen table. "Hi."

My sister threw the towel at me. "Your turn," she said as she rushed from the room.

"Okay, sure." I stood and took the now-clean pot from my mother.

My mother shook her head. "She's been riding a broomstick all day." Riding a broomstick was my mom's way of saying someone was being a bitch.

"What's up with her?"

"The baby daddy called this morning."

"Has he been paying child support?"

"Not much, and he's leaving town. The numbskull's going to Alaska to work on a fishing boat," she laughed. "Can you see that skinny little twit on a fishing boat? He can't pick up a dirty sock off the floor. How's he going to pick up a fifty-pound salmon?"

Aunt Liz walked into the kitchen smelling like Aqua Net hairspray and Jean Naté cologne. "What's that I hear about salmon? I thought we were having shepherd's pie," she said, as she sat at the table.

"We are," Mom said. "I was telling Riley about the baby daddy going to Alaska to work on a fishing boat."

Aunt Liz laughed out loud. "He won't last a week."

We all laughed but shut up fast when Angie called for Mom to help her with something.

I placed the pot on the stove, hung the towel on the oven door, and sat across from Aunt Liz. I gave her my best smile. "I need information."

Aunt Liz cocked her head to the side. "What kind of information?" she asked, sliding on her poker face.

"I know about the poker room at McGee's." Her face didn't give anything away. "And I know you're a frequent participant."

She raised an eyebrow but said nothing.

"I don't care about that. What you do for fun is your business, as long as you don't get involved with a loan shark—"

"Stop right there, little miss probation officer. I've been playing poker longer than you've been out of diapers. I know when to fold and when to walk away." She glared at me. I'd hit a nerve I hadn't meant to.

I held up my hands. "Okay. I'm sorry. I didn't mean to imply anything. Like I said, what you do for entertainment is none of my business."

"You're damn right it isn't." She crossed her arms and glared at me.

"Look, I just want some information."

"I can't tell you who attends the games."

"You make it sound like it's an AA meeting."

"It is. If anyone breaks the code of silence, they're out for good."

Apparently, my friend Sally didn't know about that rule.

I nodded. "Okay, I understand."

"What do you want to know?" She leaned back in her chair, some of her wariness dissipating.

"I'm looking for a woman named Pinky Higgins. She's not a poker player, and even if she were, your game would be way out of her price range." I leaned back in my seat. "She's the one who stole my probation car and wrecked it. My boss is pressuring me to arrest her."

"What does this have to do with my poker game?"

"I'm getting to that. Pinky associates with a lot of people who aren't exactly law-abiding citizens."

"So I gathered."

"Anyway, I talked with her mother, who gave me a list of places she may be hiding. One of the names on the list is Freddy Murphy."

Aunt Liz sat up straight. I had her attention.

She leaned in. "Freddy 'The Hands' Murphy?" Her voice barely over a whisper. Freddy Murphy was a well-known loan shark and a fence for stolen merchandise. He got his nickname because he had his hands in a lot of the criminal activity in town.

"Yes, Freddy The Hands."

"You think I know him?" She looked appalled that I would think such a thing.

"Maybe you know someone who's used his services?"

She narrowed her eyes and glared at me.

"Come on, Aunty, in all likelihood, someone at your table has lost big and needed a loan to cover their losses. They can't go to a bank, where else can they turn?"

She continued to stare.

"I've been to his house, but apparently, he stays with his girlfriend, Mindy Carr. I need her address."

She leaned back in her chair, not saying a word, but from the look on her face, I could tell the wheels in her head were spinning. I didn't know if she was thinking about who in her group of gamblers might have been desperate enough to borrow money from a loan shark or if she was debating whether she could trust me to keep mute about the confidential information she provided. I hoped she would find me trustworthy.

The timer on the stove dinged and she got up. "I'll get back to you," she said, grabbing potholders and opening the oven door. The aroma of cherries filled the air.

Ten minutes before dinner was ready, the doorbell rang. "That should be Tate," I said as Aunt Liz got up to answer the door.

Mom picked up the shepherd's pie and headed to the dining room. After placing it on the table, she smiled at me. "It's so nice that you and Tate could join us for dinner."

"Mom, I'm here every Sunday."

"I know. I'm just happy to see the two of you together."

"Don't go getting any ideas."

"You're not getting any younger, you know? It's about time you two settled down."

I gave her the evil eye but didn't say anything.

Heat rose to my cheeks when Tate walked in ahead of Aunt Liz. She wore hip-hugging black jeans and a black sweater that showed off all her curves. Her messy, sun-bleached hair looked like she'd just crawled out of bed. It made my mind wander to places I didn't need to go to while in my parents' home. Tate saw the look on my face and winked. She knew what I was thinking.

"Did you think I'd wear cutoffs and a T-shirt to dinner at your parents?"

"No," I stammered. "You look amazing."

Tate chuckled, turned to my father, and held out her hand. "Mr. Reynolds, it's nice to see you again."

He shook her hand. "Tate, you know you can call me Jim."

"Of course, Jim," she said, then turned to my mother. "Can I help?"

"Nope. Everything's ready, have a seat."

Angie walked in from the other room and gave Tate a hug. "About time you came back. I was beginning to think you didn't like us anymore."

"Nothing like that. I've been swamped at work." She looked around the room. "Where's the little guy?"

Angie took a seat across from Tate. "Jamie's at his father's. The deadbeat wants to spend time with his son before he leaves to find himself in Alaska."

"Alaska?"

Angie ladled a serving of shepherd's pie onto her plate. "Long story."

My mother passed the salad bowl to Aunt Liz and then looked at me. "Speaking of children…"

I slapped a hand over my mouth to keep from expelling a mouthful of wine across the table. "Mom, please. Don't start."

From the corner of my eye, I saw my father guzzle an entire bottle of beer without stopping to breathe. He didn't want any part of this.

My mother continued, "You two aren't getting any younger, you know."

Tate looked at me, her lips scrunched together. She was trying not to laugh.

I stared at Angie, my eyes pleading for help.

"Don't look at me. I've had one. That's my limit."

I took a big gulp from my wineglass. "Mom. We're not even living together."

"Well, why not?" She wouldn't let it go.

"I'll be going to the FBI and—"

"Riley, how many times are you going to use that excuse?"

"It's not an excuse," I protested. "I'm going."

Aunt Liz stood. "How about pie?"

"Yes, please!" Tate and my father said in unison.

Aunt Liz went to the kitchen and brought back her famous cherry pie, and vanilla ice cream. I was stuffed, but I wasn't going to pass up Aunt Liz's pie. Mom sliced and plated it, then Aunt Liz dished a scoop of ice cream onto each plate. I took my first bite, the cherries' tartness and the ice cream's sweetness caused a small moan to escape my throat. Tate looked at me and raised an eyebrow. My face reddened. I hadn't intended for anyone to hear that.

She smiled. "I think this is the best thing I've ever put in my mouth." She winked at me.

All I could think about was what I'd like to have in my mouth later that night.

CHAPTER EIGHT

Monday mornings rank low on my list of favorite days of the week. There are always a million voice mails to answer. On top of the usual Monday morning crap, today was Patty's first day of maternity leave. I liked having the office all to myself. Patty can be a little chatty, and I tease her that she must have been Chatty Cathy in another life. She claimed she wasn't old enough to know who Chatty Cathy was.

I entered my office at 7:45 and found Bud Bivens sitting at Patty's desk. To say I wasn't happy would be a colossal understatement. Without saying a word, I turned and walked to Stan's office. The door was open, so I didn't bother to knock.

Stan sat behind his desk reading the *SLO Tribune*, his mouth opened to take a bite of a breakfast burrito. I felt a strong urge to drool. I loved breakfast burritos, especially from Burrito-Burrito. Their tangy green salsa had just the right amount of spiciness. It was perfection on a tortilla.

"Stan," I said before he took a bite.

The burrito stalled an inch from his mouth, his eyes darted to mine, and his eyebrows melded. He returned the burrito to the paper plate on his desk and set the newspaper down.

"What?" he grumbled, his eyes glancing back to the burrito.

"Sorry to interrupt, but why is Bud Bivens sitting at Patty's desk?" My eyes returned to the burrito, and my mouth watered.

He took a long breath, then picked up his coffee cup and drank. "She's out for six months, and you need a partner. Hell, she may not even come back to this unit. She may want something less active for a while." He looked longingly at the burrito. I think he licked his lips, but I wasn't sure.

"What, like the court unit? She hates writing sentencing reports. AI robots could write those reports. They're mind-numbing. Writing them sucks the life out of you."

"That's why Bud's here. He needed a change of pace. He's been behind a desk for the last three years."

"Great," I huffed. "Is he even armed?"

"He went to training last week and qualifies at the range this afternoon."

"You could have given me a heads-up."

"You know as well as I do that if I'd told you ahead of time, you'd argue, and I wanted to avoid that as long as possible." He picked up the burrito. "Now, if you don't mind, I'd like to get back to my breakfast."

I could smell the roasted potatoes and scrambled eggs wafting from his desk. "Is that from Burrito-Burrito?"

"Yes." He opened his mouth, shoved a quarter of the twelve-inch burrito inside, and bit down. Wow, men had enormous mouths. He chewed and smiled at me. "Anything else?" he said with his mouth full.

I frowned, shook my head, and retreated.

When I returned to my office, Bud was on the phone, with his feet on Patty's desk. Where the hell did he think he was? In a Google office in San Francisco? I'll bet he never acted so laid-back in his tiny office in the courthouse, with the chief just down the hall. I frowned at him, and his feet dropped to the floor.

Having decided I needed a breakfast burrito from Burrito-Burrito as much as I needed oxygen, I didn't sit down. I stood at the door and waited for him to get off the phone. From what I could hear, it didn't sound like it had anything to do with work. I stood there with my arms crossed, leaning against the door frame, tapping my foot until he realized I was waiting on him.

"Hi, Riley," he said, placing the receiver back in its cradle and standing. He began walking across the room to me with his hand out. I shook it. "Looks like we'll be partners for a while."

"Yeah," I said without much enthusiasm. "I'm going to get some breakfast. I'll be back in a little bit."

"Can I come? I could use a good cup of coffee. The stuff in the break room is toxic."

He wasn't wrong. The coffeepot in the break room was ancient, and I'm pretty sure whoever bought the coffee shopped at The Grocery Outlet. Not that there's anything wrong with The Grocery Outlet, but my tastes were a little pickier when it came to coffee. He stood there like a puppy wagging his tail.

"Okay, let's go."

When we were both seated in the car, Bud asked, "So this is the car she stole?"

"Yes. This is the car Pinky stole and crashed into a truck full of shit," I said through gritted teeth.

He snapped his seatbelt. "I thought it would smell worse."

I had to laugh. I thought it would too.

The burrito gods must have been looking out for me because there was an empty space right in front of the place. I told Bud to wait in line while I walked to the corner to pay for parking. The parking attendant probably wouldn't ticket a probation vehicle, but I wasn't here on official business, so I didn't want to take a chance. When I returned, the line was out the door, but I knew from experience it would move quickly.

"I'll bet you're happy to get out of the courthouse," I said as we stood in line.

He grinned. "I think they could train a monkey to write sentencing reports. It's not exactly rocket science."

I'd never worked with Bud before and didn't know anything about him other than he had a reputation as being skilled at writing felony sentencing reports. I bet the judges weren't happy to see him reassigned. One of the biggest problems for all probation departments and law enforcement is finding people with strong writing skills. Turns out most high school graduates can't write their way out of a paper bag. Criminal justice departments across California spend a lot of time and money teaching new hires with college degrees how to write. It's even worse for those police and sheriff's departments, who don't require a college degree.

"What other units have you worked in?"

"None. I've spent all three years in the department writing reports." He frowned. "It turns out they don't want to let you leave if you're good at something. I had to talk to a union rep and get them to push for my transfer if you can believe it."

So, Bud had never been out of the office. Never worked a caseload. Never made a home call. Never done a search or an arrest. Jesus, did Stan expect me to be a training officer too? I was definitely going to have a talk with him when we got back.

Just as we got to the door, only three or four people ahead of us, a man came barreling out of the alley between Brewster's and Smokey's Deli at full speed. It was Max Maynard, and he wasn't stopping for anything, not even the line of people waiting to get into Burrito-Burrito for their morning fix. Before I could yell at him to stop, or step out of line to take him down, he charged through the crowd, pushing people out of his way and knocking a few to the ground. I started after him. Then I heard Bud yell, "Fuck!"

I looked back. He was on the ground, holding his right arm against his chest. He looked up at me. "I think my arm's broken."

I returned to his side and knelt. "Can you move it?"

He shook his head. "It hurts like hell," he said, his teeth clenched in pain.

I looked to see where Max had gone, but he was nowhere in sight. Then it dawned on me. Max came running from the alley... He might have set another fire. "Bud, I'll be right back.

Hang in there." I jogged the fifty feet to the alley. Sure enough, smoke billowed out of a dumpster. Luckily Max had again chosen a dumpster behind a brick building to set his fire.

I pulled out my cell phone, dialed 911 to report it, and asked Officer Walker to respond to the scene. They took the information, and I hung up and jogged back to Bud. The crowd had settled back in place, and Bud was standing, cradling his wrist close to his chest.

"There's a fire in a dumpster in the alley. I called 911. Fire and PD should be here soon. I can call an ambulance to take you to the hospital, or if you can wait a little while, I'll drive you. It's up to you."

"I'll wait." His eyebrows scrunched together, and his lips puckered in a grimace. "I really need a cup of coffee."

Hearing this, the guy in line near us said, "It's on me. How do you want it?"

"Black," Bud said. "Thanks."

The guy looked at me. "What about you?"

"I was going to get a breakfast burrito, no meat. But we can't accept gratuities." I pulled a twenty out of my pocket and handed it to the guy. "This should cover it."

The guy shrugged. "Okay. I'll bring it out to you."

In the distance, a siren screamed, and a few seconds later, a fire engine came around the corner of Garden Street and stopped at the alleyway. Fire personnel climbed out from several doors and went to work. The same captain from the Bubblegum Alley fire stepped out of the front seat. She looked around and spotted me. She shook her head and walked over.

"You again?" she said.

"Afraid so." I shrugged. "I was here getting a burrito, and the arsonist came running out of the alley like a bat outta hell. He knocked my partner to the ground and continued down Higuera. I lost sight of him after a block. I recognized him, so I went to look in the alley, and sure enough, the dumpster was on fire."

The captain had a quizzical look on her face. "Is it possible he knew you'd be here?"

"What? No. I didn't even know I'd be here until thirty minutes ago."

"Could he be following you?" she asked as Tate pulled up in her police unit.

I frowned but didn't say anything. I knew Max wanted to scare me, but I hadn't considered that he might be stalking me. Before I could answer, Bud walked up, holding a cup of coffee in his good hand and my burrito wedged between his elbow and his side. I reached out and took the burrito before it got any more smushed. As I started to unwrap it, Tate walked up.

"Max?" she asked, taking the burrito from me and taking a large bite.

"Hey, that's mine. Get your own." I grabbed it back before she could take another bite.

She grinned. "I know your mother taught you how to share."

"Nope, not when it comes to a burrito from Burrito-Burrito."

"Fair enough." She smiled. "So, it was Max Maynard again?"

I nodded, my mouth full of eggs, potatoes, gooey cheese, and tangy green salsa.

"We're only a few blocks from your apartment." Her forehead wrinkled.

"Shit," I said.

Bud looked at me with concern. "Why does that matter?"

Tate looked at me and pointed her thumb at Bud. "Who's he?"

"Oh, sorry." I swallowed the mouthful of burrito. "Tate, this is Bud Bivens. He's been assigned to my unit while Patty's on maternity leave. Bud, this is Detective Tate Walker."

"I'd shake your hand, but I think mine's broken," he said. "Why does it matter where her apartment is?" he asked again.

"He's after me," I said.

"What?"

"He went to prison. He blames me."

"Seriously?"

"Yeah. Now we should get you to the hospital and get that x-rayed." I wrapped up my burrito, it would have to wait. "Stan is going to kill me."

Tate let out a laugh. "How many does this make?"

I glared at her. "He's the third one, but it's not my fault."

"The third what?" Bud wanted to know.

"The third partner who's been injured with her," Tate informed him.

Bud looked at me. "Are you cursed or something?"

My glare went from Tate to him. "Shut up and get in the car. We'll call Stan on the way."

I handed what was left of my burrito to Tate. "You might as well finish it while it's hot. They're never as good reheated."

Tate took the burrito and grinned from ear to ear. "I think this means you love me."

"It means no such thing." *Did it mean something?* I glared at Bud. "I said get in the car."

CHAPTER NINE

On the way to the hospital, I called Stan. After he yelled at me for injuring another partner and asked questions about where we were when it happened, he said to report back to him after Bud had been seen by a doctor.

The emergency room wasn't crowded for a Monday morning, and shortly after we arrived, Bud was taken for an x-ray. He returned thirty minutes later. He didn't even have a chance to sit down before his name was called again, and we were escorted to a small cubicle with a pink curtain pulled around it. Bud plopped down on the tiny bed, and I leaned against the wall. A minute later, the curtain was pulled aside, and one of the most attractive women I've ever seen stepped in. Her fiery red hair cascaded down the back of her white lab coat. Before she sat on the little round stool, her steel-blue eyes took me in from head to toe, then focused on Bud.

"I'm Doctor Ross. You are Bud Bivens, correct?"

Bud nodded. "Yes, and that's my partner, Riley Reynolds. My work partner. Not my partner, partner. We're probation officers." He fumbled, trying to make it clear we weren't a couple.

"Yes, the embroidered badge on your shirt was a dead giveaway." She didn't look up as she typed on her tiny laptop.

Bud looked over her head at me, raised his shoulders, and mouthed, "Bitchy."

I smothered a laugh. *And hot.*

She looked up at Bud. "Your right wrist has a small break. You'll need a cast on it."

"For how long?"

"About six weeks." She stood. "One of the physician assistants will be in to take care of that." Without saying anything else, she walked out, the curtain swinging in the breeze.

Bud lay back on the bed, his good arm behind his head. "Talk about an ice queen. She could stop a volcano with one look."

She may be an ice queen, but she was a smokin' hot ice queen.

An hour later, we headed back to the office with a prescription for pain meds and a bright pink cast on Bud's wrist. I thought it was a little odd that he chose a pink cast, but who was I to question his choices.

"I guess I won't be going to the gun range today." He looked verklempt.

I shook my head. "I don't think so. Stan will probably send you home. At least for the rest of the day."

"Do you think they'll send me back to the courthouse?" He looked almost grief-stricken at the thought.

"Maybe. Or he'll chain you to a desk to follow up on outstanding warrants."

"Anything would be better than going back to writing reports. I was so bored out of my mind I was ready to quit."

"I've only done a few of them. It wasn't bad for the six months I was there, but any longer, and I could see how it would get mind-numbing."

Back at the office, Bud headed straight to Stan's office to learn his fate. There wasn't any yelling or crying, so I guessed Bud wasn't being sent back to the courthouse. While I waited to hear something, I checked my voice mails. Two were from police detectives wanting to know if I knew where certain wayward probationers might be hiding. If I knew, I'd probably have picked them up myself. Another message was from Pinky's mother, saying she wanted me to stop by 7-Eleven as soon as possible.

The last message had been left five minutes before I'd returned to the office, and it sent an ice-cold chill down my spine. It started with laughter. "Too bad the puny little runt got in my way. I was aiming for you, bitch. Now you know I can get to you anytime, anywhere. See you soon."

I sat there staring at the wall. Max Maynard was coming for me. I called Tate.

She answered on the first ring. "How's the junior PO?"

"His wrist is broken," I said quickly. "Tate, Maynard left a voice mail on my office phone. He was after me this morning. Bud just happened to get in his way."

"Can you play it back so I can hear it?"

I pushed the play button on the phone and held my cell phone near the speaker. His voice was cold and menacing.

When it ended, Tate said, "Have you told your boss yet?"

"No, I called you first." Then I wondered why I'd done that. Besides being the case detective, she couldn't do anything. If any of my other probationers had threatened me, I'd immediately go to Stan and inform him.

"Okay. You better go tell him."

"If I tell him, he'll restrict me to the office, and I'll be handcuffed to a desk."

Tate paused. "Better than dead, Riley."

She had a point. "Okay, I'll talk to him and write a report."

"Be sure to save the recording. We'll need it as evidence."

"Right, I'll talk to you later." I hung up and slowly walked down the hall to Stan's office. I met Bud halfway. "Well?"

"He's not sending me back to the courthouse. But I'm restricted to the office. He said I could prioritize the warrant files." He looked relieved, or he'd taken the pain meds. "How many warrant files are there?"

I chuckled. "Maybe a thousand if you count misdemeanors."

"No shit?"

"We don't care about those, so if we're only talking about felony warrants…" I paused to think about it. "Maybe three or four hundred. You should probably look for the ones that expire soon and decide if they're serious enough to get the warrant renewed or let it expire and dismiss the case."

"Okay. I'll get right on it."

"Maybe you should take the rest of the day off. Your arm has to be killing you."

"Yeah, it is. I'll knock off early."

I continued down the hall to Stan's office. Since he'd just restricted Bud from going out into the field, I decided not to go into detail about Max's threat. I needed to be out on the street asking questions, not just about Max but also about Pinky.

Stan's door was open, and he sat behind his desk reading a file. I knocked and waited for him to look up.

"What is it, Reynolds?" he grumbled without looking up. The remnants of the breakfast burrito still littered his desk.

"Stan, I had a message on my phone that's a little concerning."

He closed the file and looked at me. "About Patricia Higgins? I want her found."

"Well, there was a message from Pinky's mother asking me to stop by, but that's not the one that concerns me."

"Okay, so what did this message say?"

I took a deep breath and let it out. "It was Max Maynard."

"The arsonist?"

"Yeah, the arsonist. He said he'd intended to take me out this morning, but Bud got in the way."

"What the hell, Reynolds?"

"I don't think he was out to kill me. I think he wanted to scare me."

"Did you call your detective?"

My detective? What did he mean by that? "Yes, I called Detective Walker. I'll write up a report and save the recording as evidence. But I don't want you to go overboard and keep me off the street. I can take care of myself."

He tapped the eraser end of a pencil on his desk, his eyes focused on me. "I need to call the chief. This is getting out of hand. Don't leave the office for now."

"But, Stan—"

He held up his hand. "Just until I talk to the chief and see how he wants to handle this."

I slunk back to my office and dropped into my chair. I looked across the room at Bud, who already had a stack of files in front of him.

He looked up. "How'd it go?"

I took my jacket off, hung it over the back of my chair, and wondered why I'd given Tate the rest of my burrito. What did it say about our relationship that I handed over my barely touched burrito? Was I in love? My stomach growled. I was hungry and that made me edgy. Damn it.

"I'm stuck in the office with you until Stan talks to the chief and they decide what to do." I picked up a cheap pen and hurled it in the trash can, taking my frustration out on it. "This is bullshit. It's not my fault some A-hole is pissed and wants to get back at me for sending him to prison." I leaned on my elbows. "I didn't make him violate his probation terms. I just did my job and arrested him. What happened to him was up to the court. Why isn't he after the judge?"

"Maybe he is. Has anyone checked on him?"

"It's a her," I said. "Judge Bookings."

"Oh, the Wicked Witch of the Courthouse."

"What?"

"The Wicked Witch of the Courthouse. That's what those of us who work in the courthouse call her. Not to her face, of course."

"Why?"

Bud shook his head. "She's an absolute bitch to everyone outside her immediate staff, who she treats like family. She rails at the incompetence of every cop, and lawyers on both sides. Probation officers are treated like dog shit on the bottom of her shoe. And I don't say that because she's a woman. We had names for all the judges we didn't like. We called Judge Billings the Bastard on the Bench."

He said it just as I took a sip of coffee, and I sprayed a little across my desk. I grabbed napkins out of a drawer and began wiping it up.

He laughed. "But The Witch is the worst. Having to appear in her courtroom is like entering a torture chamber. You know you won't get out unscathed. Even the most seasoned officers take a beating. She finds any reason to criticize a report: a single misspelled word, a missing comma, or a poorly phrased sentence. Heaven forbid she doesn't like a sentencing recommendation you make. Even if it's a mandatory sentence required by statute, and you have no choice but to recommend it. If she disagrees, she goes full-blown apeshit. One time she ordered the chief to appear in her courtroom and explain why everyone in his department was so incompetent."

"Are you kidding me?" I had no idea. I knew some judges thought they were special, and their shit didn't stink, but apparently I didn't realize some were over-the-top egomaniacs.

"No. I'm not." He leaned back in his black, fake-leather chair. The county was way too cheap to buy real leather chairs. Mine had a few pieces of duct tape holding it together. "You know she's family, right?"

I knew the judge was a lesbian, but obviously, she and I didn't run in the same circles. But more importantly...*Family*? Did Bud just come out to me? Was my gaydar on the fritz? How did I miss this?

"Yes, I know the judge is queer, although she'd never use such a crude term to describe herself." I cocked my head to the side and looked at him. "You're gay?"

A huge smile lit up his face. "Girl, I'm as queer as a three-dollar bill," he said in a perfect imitation of the late Leslie Jordan. He held up his right arm. "Would a straight man choose a bright-pink cast?"

I shook my head. "Well, I'll be damned. I had no idea. And I've never heard a whisper around the office about you."

He shrugged. "I'm not in the closet. But I don't bring it up at work. The courthouse is a breeding ground of conservativism. Is there something in the water at law school that makes them lean Republican?"

I laughed. "Maybe they hand out red Kool-Aid to the ones who want to be prosecutors or work at big prestigious firms who only care about billable hours and raking in the money."

"You might be right. The poor serfs in the public defender's office, toiling away in the basement, don't seem to have been affected."

"Yeah, they definitely get the short end of the stick," I said. "And I get that they believe everyone is entitled to a defense, but how can they represent people they know are guilty and do their best to get them off?"

"I dated Jimmy Smith for a while. Nice guy, but I could never understand how he could do his damnedest to get killers and thieves off."

"Is that why you stopped dating him?"

"Oh nooo." He shook his head from side to side. "We stopped seeing each other after a big hairy bear came along and scooped him up."

A "bear" in gay lingo is a big hairy man who likes smaller, not so hairy men. I started to laugh just as my phone rang. I picked up the receiver and put it to my ear.

"Reynolds," I said, sounding as professional as possible.

"It's Pinky." Pinky was twenty, but her high-pitched squeaky voice made her sound like she was ten.

I sat up in my chair. "Pinky, where are you?"

"I have to get out of town. They're after me," she said, her voice clipped.

"Pinky, who's after you?"

"Lester Knight."

"Where are you? I'll come get you."

"I can't come in, Riley. I wouldn't be safe in jail. He knows people inside."

"Pinky, I can talk to the district attorney. They can find you a safe place to stay."

"No, Riley, nowhere here is safe."

"Where will you go?"

"Mexico, or maybe Canada. Maybe the Cayman Islands." She tried to laugh.

"But Pinky—"

"No, Riley, I have to go. Tell my mother and Trixie I'll be back when it's safe. Riley, you have to make sure he doesn't hurt either one of them. Okay?"

"Listen, Pinky—" The line went dead. "Damn it!"

"Who's Pinky?" Bud asked.

"The chick who stole my car."

"She's not willing to turn herself in?"

I shook my head. "She said Lester Knight's after her."

"Lester Knight, the gang leader?"

I nodded.

"Where is she?"

"She wouldn't say." I stood and pulled on my jacket.

"Where are you going? Aren't you supposed to stay put?"

"I'm hungry. Stan can't keep me from taking a break."

Bud walked toward the door. "I need a break, too." He shoved his good arm into his jacket sleeve.

"Look, Bud, if you've taken any pain pills, you should stay here. If anything happens and you're on meds, there would be hell to pay."

"I haven't taken any yet. And besides, we're going on a break, right? We're not going looking for trouble."

"Well, if trouble accidentally finds us, you better stay out of the way. You're not armed, remember?"

A frown crossed his face. "I know. I should be at the range as we speak," he said just as Stan walked out of his office and saw us headed for the door.

"Where in the hell do you two think you're going?" I could tell he was trying not to raise his voice and cause a scene in the office.

"Stan, it's past lunchtime. We're going to get something to eat. If that's okay with you." I gave him my best smile to cover the fact that lunch wasn't the only thing on my agenda.

He glared at me. "Riley, you're already on the chief's shit list. Don't make it any worse."

I tried to look innocent. "Stan, we're only going to lunch. Don't worry so much. Have some faith in me."

His forehead wrinkled, and I could tell by his jaw that he was grinding his teeth.

"Besides, Bud's a Boy Scout. He wouldn't let me get into any trouble."

"Working with you, he won't be a Boy Scout for long," Stan muttered and walked back into his office, forgetting all about whatever he had planned to do a minute ago.

Bud looked at me, disappointment on his face. "A Boy Scout? Really? That's the best you could come up with?"

"I was under pressure. He caught me off guard," I said as I opened the door and held it for him to exit.

"Oh, so you're the chivalrous type of dyke, aye?"

"Shut up, asshole. Your arm's broken. I was being nice."

That would be the last time I tried to do something nice for him, the ingrate.

CHAPTER TEN

"Do you like Del Monte Café?" I asked.

"Sure, what's not to like?"

I pulled out of the parking lot onto Bishop Street and headed to the train station on Santa Barbara Avenue. Del Monte Café was a hundred-year-old building that may have been a church or schoolhouse at one time. The food was just like your grandmother would make—mouth-watering, nothing fancy, no frills, and portions as big as your head. I never left there without a doggy bag.

It was 1:30 when we pulled into an empty space on a side street. The lunch crowd had thinned, and we had no problem getting a table as soon as we walked in. A minute later, our waitress, Betty, arrived with two glasses of water. Betty was no spring chicken and had worked at the café for as long as I could remember. She looked like a drill sergeant and had a raspy smoker's voice.

"The lunch special is a chili burger with fries or salad." She looked at Bud skeptically. "Who's your friend, Riley? You decide to switch to the other side of the plate?" Betty's daughter was gay and a friend of mine, so it was no secret to her which team I played for.

I laughed. "Betty, this is Bud. He's taking Patty's place until she returns from maternity leave. And no, I haven't switched teams. Bud's a friend of Dorothy's."

Betty made an odd face. "Who's Dorothy?"

Bud and I laughed. "It's a code gay men use. It means they're gay."

"They'd say they're a friend of Dorothy's?"

Bud nodded.

Betty pulled her notepad out of her apron pocket. "Learn something new every day. What can I get you?"

I ordered breakfast, I loved the corned beef hash and poached eggs with hash browns. Bud ordered a cheeseburger and fries. I'd warned him to stay away from the chili, or he'd be walking back to the office.

When Betty left, Bud asked how my weekend had gone, and I made the mistake of telling him about the Sex on the Beach cocktails with Tate. He laughed, teasing that I'd had sex on the beach with a cop. At the time Tate and I were drinking them, I didn't think about how it might sound. But now I did see the humor in it. I also wondered what it would be like to have actual sex on the beach with Tate. Starting with the way she kissed me, gently at first, her tongue seeking entry, then our tongues wildly doing the tango. Her lips nipping on my neck, leaving a mark, claiming me as hers. Her hands cupping my breasts, squeezing my nipples, driving me crazy with need. Tate laying on top of me, our pussies grinding together as we kissed roughly, then Tate slowly kissing her way down my stomach to my—

"Riley." Bud's nudge on my knee stopped that fantasy dead in its tracks. "Hey, where'd you go?"

I blinked away thoughts of a naked Tate on the beach. "Sorry, just work stuff. Nothing important." I hoped my face wasn't red, as it had gotten hot inside the restaurant all of a sudden.

When we were done we swung by 7-Eleven to see what information Pinky's mother had for me. Traffic downtown was light, and we arrived before the afterschool rush at 3:15. Lena was restocking Big Gulp cups near the soda machine when we entered.

"Hi, Lena," I said. "This is Officer Bivens. He's working with me while Patty's on leave."

"When's her baby due?" she asked.

"Four weeks."

She shook her head. "Kids. The bane of our existence."

I didn't have a reply to that since I didn't have any. "So, Lena, your message said you had some additional places Pinky might be hiding out?"

She nodded. "If she hasn't already taken off for parts unknown."

"Yeah, she called earlier and said she was leaving town. I need to find her before she does."

"She could be halfway to Mexico by now." Lena pulled a piece of paper from her pocket and handed it to me. "I found these names in Pinky's room. They don't have addresses, but I'm guessing you have ways to find that out."

I recognized the first name on the list—Harry Mack, a small-time bookie. He'd been in jail for the last six months, so it was unlikely he knew anything.

The other name, coincidentally, was Mindy Carr.

"Great, thanks, Lena. We'll check out these names." I pocketed the slip of paper as a teenager walked in, setting off the bell. "We'll let you get back to work."

"Okay. You'll let me know if you find her, right?"

"Absolutely." I opened the glass door and walked out as several more teens approached for their afternoon sugar fix.

As we settled in the car, Bud asked, "Do you know either of the names?"

"Yeah. Harry Mack's in jail for operating a gambling den without a license. The other name is Mindy Carr. She's Freddy Murphy's girlfriend."

"The loan shark?"

I nodded. "From what his friends say, he likes to think of himself as an entrepreneur."

Bud laughed. "That's a good one."

"I have some feelers out on Mindy and Freddy. Hopefully, I'll have something soon."

When we got back to the office, Stan's car wasn't in the lot, so I left early. It was four o'clock on a Monday and I had nowhere to be and no idea what to do, so I called Tate because…why not?

She answered on the first ring. "Stolen car or lost gun?"

"Not funny. Can't I just call my gir—" I stopped midsentence. *Girlfriend?* I hadn't thought we were that serious. But neither of us was seeing anyone else, so did that mean we were exclusive? A couple?

"Were you about to say *girlfriend?*"

"No, of course not. We aren't, are we?"

Tate didn't answer right away. "You know, I'm not really in a place where I can talk about this. I'm just leaving a briefing on Max Maynard."

I could hear commotion and voices in the background.

"How about I pick up Chinese and come by later?" she said.

I knew where we'd end up if she came over, and I was all for sex with Tate. But did I want to have a deep, serious discussion about our relationship? Didn't I have enough going on in my life at the moment?

"Sure. Don't forget soy sauce. I'm out."

Tate laughed. "You've been out for six months. Maybe we should go grocery shopping."

Did she say "we" should go grocery shopping? "Yeah, sure. I'll see you later."

I pulled up in front of my apartment twenty minutes later. Mike was out front pruning the bushes. He did it weekly. It was like they were bonsai trees, and he sculpted them within an inch of their lives. His back was to me, and I could tell by how he swung his butt and hips that he had earbuds in. I walked around the stairs, into his line of sight, and waved to get his attention.

He pulled an earbud out of one ear. "Riley, sweetheart. How are you?" he sang in a soprano voice.

I leaned in and kissed him on the cheek. "I'm good, Mike."

"You're home early. Everything okay?"

"Yeah. I left early. I've been working my ass off."

"How's that hot girlfriend of yours?" He smiled mischievously.

"Tate isn't…" I stopped. Is she? I guess we'd come to an understanding tonight. "Tate's good. She's on her way over, as a matter of fact."

"Well, give her a kiss for me." He put the earbud back in his ear.

I nodded and started up the stairs. It was warm inside my apartment. I'd double-checked that all the windows were closed and locked when I left that morning. I walked around, opened windows to let the breeze in, and then focused on getting Randolph fed. When I opened the top of the fish food container, I swear he smiled at me.

"How's it going, Randolph? How was your day?" I sprinkled the red and orange flakes across the top of the water. More interested in his dinner than a conversation with me, he swam off to chase down the bits.

Feeling unappreciated, I entered the bedroom, changed into a comfortable pair of red sweatpants and a Fresno State T-shirt. I returned to the kitchen and pulled a SLO Stout from the refrigerator. Tate wouldn't be around for another two hours, so I curled up on the couch to finish reading my Kat Jackson book.

I woke up to someone pounding on the door. I crossed the room and checked the peephole to make sure it was Tate. It was, and she held a brown bag in her arms. I opened the door and reached for the bag.

There was a frown on her face. "Were you asleep? I was about ready to knock down the door."

"Yeah, I was reading and must have dozed off." I headed into the kitchen, Tate behind me.

"I was worried when you didn't answer the door." Lines were etched on her forehead, and her eyebrows scrunched together. She reached out and stroked my cheek.

I blushed. "I'm sorry. I must have been really out."

She leaned in and kissed my cheek, then looked into my eyes. When I didn't look away, she gently placed her lips on mine. Electricity shot down my center and I moaned but pulled back.

"Tate, as much as I like that, the food smells amazing, and I'd like to eat it while it's still hot, not reheated in the microwave."

She smiled, her eyes hooded. "Okay, let's eat, then talk," she said. "We're going to have a serious conversation tonight, right?"

I swallowed. I wasn't sure I was ready for "the talk."

"Help yourself to a beer. There's stout and some kind of pale ale." I took the white cardboard containers out of the bag, carried them into the living room, and sat on the couch.

The sun was setting, and the sky was turning various shades of pink and orange. I opened a container of orange chicken and stuck a fork in but didn't take a bite. I watched Tate open the other container. She stuck chopsticks in, pulled out a shrimp, guided it into her mouth, and smiled at me. I looked at the beautiful picture outside my window and wondered why I was so conflicted about my feelings for her. We'd been seeing each other for close to four years. We'd taken two breaks. Tate had gone out with a few other women during those breaks, but according to her, she hadn't slept with any of them. I'd gone on a few dates with a dispatcher at the sheriff's department, but it never got serious or sexual. In the end, Tate and I always found ourselves back together. I knew her like the back of my hand, and I liked the feeling.

Deep down I knew I was the problem. I was the one who had issues. Maybe I needed to see a shrink. Hmm, something to think about.

"Riley." Tate's voice and another nudge on my knee brought me back to the present, and I looked at her. God, she was beautiful, the rays of the setting sun in the front window gave her hair a bright golden glow, and her ice-blue eyes sent shockwaves to the parts of my body that were already aroused.

I shook myself. "Sorry, what did you say?" I plucked a piece of chicken from the container and smiled.

"I asked if you'd like a shrimp." She held out her chopsticks, a shrimp pinched between them.

"Yes, please." I leaned in and opened my mouth. She guided the shrimp in, and I closed my lips around the chopsticks as she slowly withdrew them.

I moaned in pleasure. "That's so good." I plucked a piece of chicken and held it out to her. "Chicken?" I said, trying to sound seductive.

She leaned in, closed her lips around the fork, closed her eyes, and slowly pulled away. "Oh, my God, that is so good," she said, wiping her mouth with the back of her hand. "How about we trade containers every three bites?"

"Deal," I said, taking another bite of orange chicken.

Two bites later we traded. I couldn't decide which was better: the orange chicken, the sweet and sour shrimp, or how she looked at me like I was on the menu.

She let out a sigh and placed her container on the coffee table. "Riles, I want to tear your clothes off right now, but we need to talk."

Talk? "I thought we were talking."

She leaned forward and put a hand on my leg. "Riley, what are we doing?"

Oh, shit. We were doing this.

"Ummmm." I tried not to squirm. "Doing?"

"Damn it, Riley." She pulled away. "Are we going anywhere, or are we just two friends who fuck?"

I cringed. I tried to hide the deer-in-the-headlights feeling that was overtaking me. I had to think. I did want to be with her, but I was afraid of a long-term commitment. I thought we were on the same page, but now she wanted more. And she was starting to use the L word. It scared the shit out of me. Logically I knew my fear went back to feelings of not being good enough and being dumped or betrayed. My brain knew Tate wouldn't cheat on me like my ex had. Tate was loyal, reliable, responsible. Hell, she owned a house. We spent almost all our free time and most of our nights together. But a part of me saw Tate as out of my league. I didn't know what she saw in me. Maybe I couldn't commit because I didn't think I was enough. Inside I was still that scrawny, flat-chested girl with glasses who never understood why Tate had kissed her in the locker room. Eventually she'd want someone prettier, sexier. I saw how other women looked at her, the winks and silent invitations they gave her. It triggered my insecurities over and over again.

I let out a breath I didn't realize I'd been holding, set the container of shrimp on the coffee table and took her hand. "Tate, I'm not interested in anyone else." I looked down at our hands. "But I still want to join the FBI." I couldn't think of any other reason to give her.

"Do you? Or is that just an excuse?" Her lips formed a thin line, and her left eyebrow raised in a question.

I didn't know what to say.

"Riles, I've been in love with you since that first kiss in high school."

My head spun. I blinked multiple times, not sure I heard her correctly. "What? Why are you just telling me this? Why did you ignore me after you kissed me?"

Her chin dropped to her chest. "You scared the shit out of me back then."

I narrowed my eyes. "I don't understand."

She raised her head. Her eyes were wet with unshed tears. "I wasn't as confident as I pretended to be. That was all an act. I was just as scared and insecure as every other high school kid. I knew I wasn't good enough for you. You were so smart. I knew you would leave town and go to college somewhere, then on to something big. I didn't have anything to offer to make you want to stay. So, I pretended the kiss meant nothing. I put on an act. I was a senior, and you were just a junior, so not worth my time." A tear rolled down her cheek.

"Wait. What?" I was confused. "You didn't think you were good enough? I thought I wasn't good enough and that's why you ignored me."

She squeezed my hand "I'm so sorry I made you feel—"

Her phone rang, interrupting our long-needed discussion.

She looked at the screen. "Fuck, it's work." She wiped the tear from her face. "I have to take it."

I nodded.

"Walker," she said, hiding any trace of emotion. "Shit. Okay, I'll be right there." She ended the call, shoved the phone into her back pocket, and stood. "I'm sorry. I have to go. There's been another fire." She picked up the empty beer bottle and the container of orange chicken and walked to the kitchen.

I got up and followed her. "Where?"

"Two blocks from here, behind the liquor store on Marsh."

"Mr. Archer's store?"

Mr. Archer had owned Archer Liquor and Deli for as long as I could remember. It was a favorite place for kids on their way to and from the high school.

"Yeah. I don't have any details." She pulled me into a hug.

"He's getting close," I whispered, my head nestled in the crook of her neck.

She hugged me tighter and kissed the top of my head. "I know." She let go and headed toward the door, stopping to take her jacket from the coat rack. "Have you told Mike what's going on?"

"I'll go fill him in." I wrapped my arms around her waist. "Be careful."

"I will." She leaned down and claimed my lips in a kiss that said we were more than friends with benefits, and at that minute, I couldn't disagree.

When the kiss ended, she backed away and reached for the doorknob. "I'll call as soon as I can."

I nodded, not trusting my voice.

She opened the door and ran down the stairs, taking them two at a time. I walked to the window and watched her pull on her helmet, climb onto her motorcycle and take off down the street. It was dark, and there wasn't a streetlight out front. As I stood there, I noticed someone standing two houses down on the opposite side of the street. From the outline I could tell it was a woman. She looked familiar. Then it hit me, it was Pinky. I bolted out the door, down the stairs and out to the street. She was gone. It would be fruitless to chase after her. I knew Pinky. She was like an elf or a fairy and could disappear in the blink of an eye.

CHAPTER ELEVEN

I trudged back up the stairs, then remembered my promise to talk to my landlord. I grabbed a jacket off the coat rack, pocketed my keys, and set off down the stairs again. As I crossed the driveway to Mike's back door, I could hear music. It was Cher, "If I Could Turn Back Time," to be exact. As I approached the kitchen window, I spotted him holding a wooden spoon in place of a microphone and singing along. I waited for the song to end before knocking on the door. He looked out the window, smiled when he saw it was me and motioned for me to enter.

No longer holding his faux microphone, he met me just inside the door and enveloped me in a warm hug. "What brings you by?"

"I wish it was just to hang out and dish, but I have a situation."

He returned to the kitchen and grabbed a bottle of tequila off the counter. "Have a seat. I'll pour." He went to the cabinet next to the refrigerator, took down two shot glasses. He placed one in front of me and filled it. "So what is it? Backed-up toilet, clogged disposal?" He sat on the stool on the other side of the counter and poured tequila into his tiny glass.

I could feel my forehead wrinkle and my eyebrows scrunching together. "No. The apartment is fine. It's great." I lifted the shot glass. "Sláinte."

"What the hell does that mean?" He looked at me like I had a screw loose.

I tossed back the tequila, swallowed, then coughed. It burned going down. "It's Irish. It means good health."

"Okay, good health to us both." He raised the little glass and poured the tequila into his mouth, swallowed, and grimaced. "Shit, I forgot the salt and lime." He jumped up, grabbed a lime, knife, shaker of salt and returned to the table. "If it's not the apartment, what is it?" He began slicing a lime into little wedges. When he was done, he moved the cutting board to where we could both reach it.

I picked up a lime wedge and bit into it. The tartness made my mouth pucker. "I have a work-related problem that may have followed me home."

"That sounds troubling. What kind of problem?"

I told him about the fires and Max but didn't say his last name for confidentiality reasons. Although he was the primary suspect in the fires, it might not be public knowledge yet. I'd need to ask Tate if his name had been released to the media. Then I told him Max had made several threats involving me.

Mike slammed his shot glass down on the table, upsetting the bottle of tequila. I grabbed it before it fell over.

"What the hell?" He took the bottle from me and refilled my glass, then his. "I don't get it. Why you?"

"Several years ago, he was sent to prison. He blames me." I poured salt onto the edge of my hand in the V between my thumb and index finger.

"Even I know it's the judge who orders that. Why is he blaming you?"

I sucked the salt off my hand, drank the tequila, and quickly bit into the lime. This time it didn't make my mouth pucker as much. "I'm the one who arrested him for violating his probation.

I told the court he was a danger to the community and should be sent to prison." I shrugged. "I've done the same thing dozens of times with other probationers, and it's never come back to haunt me." I picked up a discarded lime wedge and squeezed it. "Until now."

Mike laid his hand on top of mine and patted it. "Sweety, this isn't your fault. You did your job. This guy's an asshole who's never taken responsibility for his shit. He blames everyone else for his shitty lot in life."

I tried to smile, but knew it didn't reach my eyes. "I know. But now he's focused on me, which could endanger you and my family." My shoulders sagged. "I could have Tate request police protection. They could assign a unit out front if you want."

Mike walked over to the tall cabinet where he kept an ironing board and broom. He opened the door, reached in, and pulled out an aluminum baseball bat. "There's one here, one behind the front door, and a third under my bed, and I have a Saturday night special in my nightstand."

I'm sure the shocked look on my face amused him.

"Babyface, I'm an old drag queen. I've had to learn the hard way about self-defense." He put the bat back in the closet and returned to the table.

"Is the gun registered? Do you know how to use it?" I couldn't picture him holding a gun, let alone firing it.

He chuckled. "Yes, to both questions. Before you moved in, I dated a soldier at Camp SLO. He took me to the gun range and taught me how to use it. We went several times while he was stationed here." He chuckled. "I felt so butch."

I barked out a laugh. Mike was anything but butch.

He lifted the bottle of tequila. "One more?"

I shook my head. "No, I better not. I should get home. I don't have my phone, and Tate might call. If I don't answer she'll worry." We both stood and I reached out and hugged him.

"She's a good one, Riley. Don't you go screwing it up," he said, his tone serious. "You do everything you can to keep her."

I was stunned and didn't know what to say, so I just smiled.

"Make sure all your doors and windows are locked and call me if you see anyone strange around the neighborhood. Okay?"

"Yes, ma'am." He gave me a mock salute.

I kissed him on the cheek and returned to my empty apartment. The door was unlocked. In my hurry to catch Pinky, I'd forgotten to lock it. To be safe, I retrieved my pepper spray from the kitchen drawer and went through the apartment room by room to make sure no one had snuck in while I'd been shooting tequila with Mike. It took all of two minutes. I returned to the kitchen and put the pepper spray back in the drawer and leaned against it. Feeling a little buzzed from the tequila, I thought I better eat something to soak it up. I opened the refrigerator and grabbed the orange chicken. I detested cold leftovers, including pizza. If the goddess had intended humans to eat cold food, they would never have invented fire or microwaves. I popped the chicken in the microwave and set it to heat for sixty seconds. While I waited, I filled a tall glass with water, drank it down, and refilled it. The last thing I would need in the morning was a dehydration headache.

When the timer dinged, I removed the plate, grabbed a fork, plopped down on the couch, and glanced out the window. Pinky stood across the street again, looking up at my apartment. I wasn't sure she could see me, so I raised my hand and waved. She waved back then jogged off down the street.

What the hell was she up to? Why was she watching me? For some reason, her hanging around didn't scare me. I knew Pinky wasn't out to hurt me. Max, on the other hand, was a different matter. I think he intended to kill me. But Pinky was different. She was almost like an annoying little sister you love but drives you crazy. In any case, she was gone now.

Pounding on my door woke me from my place on the couch. It seemed it was becoming a thing. My heart pounded from being abruptly awakened. I looked at my watch; it was eleven o'clock. Tate had been gone for four hours. I went to the door and looked out the peephole. Tate stood there. She looked wiped out.

I opened the door, and she went straight to the refrigerator without saying a word. "I'm starving."

I walked up behind her and pushed her away. "Go. Sit. I'll heat the Chinese food."

She sat at the kitchen table. "I don't need it heated."

The thought of cold, congealed shrimp and gooey orange chicken almost made me gag, and I shook my head. "It'll only take sixty seconds," I said. "Do you want a beer?"

She nodded, looking too tired to use her words.

I placed the heaping plate of sweet and sour shrimp and orange chicken in the microwave and set the timer. Then I reached into the refrigerator, took out a SLO Stout, twisted off the top, and handed it to her. She gave me a brief smile, raised the bottle slightly. "Cheers," she said before guzzling half of it down.

She set the bottle on the table just as the timer dinged. I took the plate out of the microwave and grabbed a fork—she was way too tired to safely operate chopsticks. I placed the food in front of her.

"I'm guessing you didn't catch him." I sat down across from her.

She speared a shrimp and brought it to her mouth. She closed her eyes and shook her head to signal that they hadn't. "Same MO as the other fires. It was set in the dumpster behind Mr. Archer's store. Unfortunately, the building isn't brick like the others. There was a lot of damage this time, and Mr. Archer and his wife live above the store. Luckily, they weren't home. His son was working in the store. He smelled smoke and called 911, but by the time the fire department got there, the whole back of the store and the stairs up to the second floor were in flames." She took a deep breath, let it out, and shoveled in another forkful of shrimp.

"Fuck!" I slammed my fist on the table, and Tate's head jerked up in surprise. "Fuck. Fuck. Fuck." Tears filled my eyes. "That poor family." I reached for Tate's napkin and wiped my face. "Why is this happening?"

She put down her food and put her hand on top of mine, just like Mike had done a few hours earlier. "It's not your fault."

I tossed the napkin in the trash. "Mike said the same thing. But Max is doing this to get back at me. People are getting hurt because this maniac wants to get back at me."

She took my hand in both of hers and leaned in, her head only inches away from mine. "We'll catch him, Riley."

I looked into her eyes. "Before he kills someone?"

She let go of my hand and picked up her fork. "We're trying, Riley. The whole department is on alert. The chief assigned two more patrol units to the area, so there's around-the-clock presence. It's just a matter of time. We'll get him."

I nodded and looked over at Randolph swimming in circles in his little water and glass home. Oh, to be a goldfish without a care in the world, except when your next meal would drop from the sky.

CHAPTER TWELVE

The other side of the bed was empty when the alarm went off at six thirty the next morning. Tate hadn't made a sound when she left, and I wondered if she'd gotten any sleep. After I showered, dressed, and dropped a few flakes in Randolph's bowl, I headed out the door. Just as I was about to get in my car, my phone beeped, alerting me to a text message. I climbed in and brought up the message. It was from my aunt.

121 East Second Street.

There was no need to put a name to it. I knew it was Mindy Carr's address. I sent a heart emoji back and started my car.

Since I hadn't eaten breakfast, I stopped at the donut shop on Broad Street. I picked out a couple of glazed donuts and a coffee, then stopped at the office to switch to my probation car. Coffee in one hand and donuts on the seat next to me, I headed to Second Street, hoping to catch Freddy at his girlfriend's.

Freddy Murphy operated as both a bookie and a loan shark. His behind-closed-doors dealings had brought him a certain level of success. With that success, he'd acquired many upscale clients, mainly high-stakes gamblers. Because he rubbed elbows with influential people, he thought he was invincible, and to some extent, he was. He knew politicians and wealthy businesspeople and had dirt on them all. He knew what closets they kept their skeletons in and where they buried their bodies.

That's why the address Aunt Liz gave me didn't make sense. 121 East Second Street was in one of the poorest sections of town. I would have thought he'd put his girlfriend up in a fancier hood.

When I pulled up in front of the dilapidated puke-green single-story house, a black pit bull lay on the ground, chained to a metal pole in the grassless front yard. I instantly despised the guy. Surprisingly the dog didn't bark. It just lay there, eyeing me as I walked up the cracked concrete path. Despite the house's poor condition, the front porch was surprisingly clean, and a welcome mat lay in front of the door. I climbed the three steps and knocked on the door. After a few moments, it opened. Unfortunately for Freddy, he had a face that matched his occupation. He resembled a weasel. His beady eyes darted around nonstop, and his pointed nose stuck out like the end of an ice cream cone, and the dark gray bags under his eyes were nearly as big as my aunt's pocketbook. It goes without saying he was not an attractive man.

He chewed on a toothpick as he looked over my shoulder at my probation car parked at the curb. "You here for a loan?" he asked, one eyebrow arched.

I shook my head and pulled my jacket back enough to expose my badge. "I'm Officer Reynolds with the probation department."

"Yeah, the car gave you away," he chuckled.

"Can I come in?"

He had an amused expression on his face. "Sure, why not? You're not the first probation officer to find themselves in need of my services."

That was interesting, and I wondered who in the department was desperate enough to go to a loan shark.

I stepped into the house and looked around. The furnishings looked expensive, and two of the biggest televisions I'd ever seen hung on the living room walls.

He nodded to the televisions. "I like to watch sports."

"So I've heard."

"How much do you need?" He picked up a pack of Lucky Strikes from the coffee table and shook one out. I wondered if it was just a coincidence that he smoked that brand or if he thought it reinforced his image as a lucky SOB.

I shook my head. "That's not why I'm here. I'm looking for Pinky Higgins. I heard she might be here."

He took a deep drag from his cigarette, exhaling slowly before answering. "Pinky? Yeah, she was here, but she left last night." He paused, considering his words. "She in some sort of trouble? She said she was leaving town."

"Did she say where she was headed?"

He raised his shoulders and scrunched up his lips in thought. "She might have said something about Mexico being nice this time of year."

I put my hands in my pockets and tried to look casual. "Do you mind if I look around?" I knew the chances he'd say yes were slim to none, but you never know. Criminals aren't the sharpest tools in the shed.

He chuckled, then took another drag off the cigarette. "I'm not on probation. So, unless you have a warrant, I think you already know the answer."

I shrugged. "I had to take a shot."

He laughed. "I'd have been disappointed if you hadn't."

I thanked him for his time and took my leave. As I walked back to my car, the pit bull stood. Its tail wagged as it walked toward me, stopping short of the path when the chain ran out. I continued to my car, opened the passenger door, and grabbed the sack from the bakery and a bottle of water from the trunk. I pulled out a donut and tossed it to the dog. He inhaled it in one large slobbery bite, then looked at me expectantly. I laughed and threw him the second donut. What the hell? He probably needed it more than my waistline did. "That's all I got, big guy,"

I said as I emptied the water into a metal bowl that had seen better days.

When I got back to the office, there was a message on my desk to report to Stan's office. I turned to go when my personal phone vibrated in my back pocket. I exhaled, thankful for the momentary reprieve. I looked at the screen but didn't recognize the number. "Hello?"

"Riley, it's me. Pinky."

I sat on the corner of my desk. "Pinky? How did you get my personal number?"

She chuckled. "I lifted your business card from my mom's purse. It was written on the back."

"I see. What are you up to? Why have you been hanging around my apartment?" I looked out my office window to see if she was nearby. I didn't see her anywhere. "Where are you?"

"I'm at my mom's, but don't hurry over. I won't be here long. I know you saw me last night, and I didn't want you to think I was going to boost your car or break into your apartment." She paused. "And I'm sorry about your car. I was just trying to mess with you. It was a joke. I was going to leave it a few blocks away. But the cop saw me and started chasing me, and it got out of hand."

"I'll say."

"I said I was sorry."

"Okay, but why are you hanging around my apartment? What are you up to?"

"I was just keeping an eye on the place. I saw that guy who's been setting the fires and followed him. He's been watching you."

A chill ran down my spine. "I know." I paused. "I thought you left town."

"I did, but I came back. I couldn't leave my mom and Trixie to deal with my mess. I need to handle my own shit." She paused. "Anyway, about cleaning up my mess. Would your girlfriend want information about some big shit going down? If I help her, maybe, we can call it even?"

Again, with the girlfriend thing. Was the universe sending me a message? "Who does it involve?"

"Lester Knight."

"So, helping the cops might also save your ass."

"Yeah, something like that."

"I'll see what she thinks. Call me tomorrow morning," I said. "And Pinky…"

"Yeah."

"Try not to do anything illegal in the meantime. Keep your head down."

She laughed. "I'll do my best, but a leopard can't change its spots." Then the line went dead.

Well, crap. What kind of game was she playing?

I slid my butt off my desk and went down the hall to see what Stan wanted. Without even saying good morning, he demanded I find Pinky. He was allowing overtime to surveil her mother's house. Since Patty was on maternity leave and Bud had a broken arm, he'd assign someone to work with me.

Stakeouts are the worst possible assignment. Boring as hell, stuck in a car, usually with some idiot who hadn't showered and had eaten a bean burrito for lunch, then farted all afternoon. Tonight was no exception. If I had any doubt about whether or not Stan was still miffed at me for the shitty car fiasco, it was made crystal clear when I found Jack McCarthy, Max's parole agent waiting for me in the parking lot. Not only was Jack a misogynist, he was big and hairy, and he smelled like he'd been living in a cave in the forest all winter. His long black hair dripped with enough grease to fry an egg. If the hair on his face were white, he could have had a side gig as a mall Santa, except the lingering odor of reindeer dung would end their childish dreams of Xboxes, Power Rangers, and Pretty Ponies and send the kids and their parents running for the exits in fear that Master of the Universe supervillain Stinkor had invaded Santa's body. On a personal note, I worried that the clothes I'd worn would have to be bagged and burned. There wasn't enough laundry soap in the county to get that smell out.

We'd been sitting in Jack's unmarked parole car a few houses from Pinky's mother's since late morning. It was now close to ten p.m. It had been a miserable day, and I was running out of patience. I rolled the window down and stuck my nose out in search of fresh air. As if things couldn't get any worse, Jack lit a cigarette. That was the final straw.

"It's almost ten. I think we need to pack it in," I said, trying not to breathe in the toxic fumes.

Jack blew out a stream of smoke that seemed to have no end, then flicked the ash of his cigarette on the floor of the state-owned car. "Why? Late night is when the action happens. Everybody goes home eventually. Just watch. She'll show up in a few hours."

A few hours? I looked at the clueless idiot and shook my head. "Nope, I'm done. I've put in my eight hours, and Stan hates overtime."

He laughed and took another drag from his cigarette. "Stan's a pussy. I'm stayin'."

God, I hate when men use that word. When a woman uses it, it can be a beautiful thing, but when it comes out of a man's mouth, it's just plain offensive.

I opened the door and climbed out. "Fine, you do that. But I'm done for the day."

He tossed the lit cigarette out his window, and sparks flew like tiny fireworks when it hit the ground. "No skin off my nose." He leaned his head back, crossed his arms, and closed his eyes.

I slammed the door shut, knowing he'd fall asleep for a few hours and claim overtime. He was a piece of work, and there was nothing I could do about it. If I ratted him out, I'd be on the outs, labeled a snitch. If I didn't, he'd rake in overtime pay he didn't deserve. I hated fucking rocks and hard places.

Since I'd gone on the stakeout with Jack, I'd have to find a way back to my car in the office parking lot on the other side of town. It was dark, and although SLO is a relatively safe city, and I was armed, I didn't really want to walk five miles alone in the dark. So that left me with two options: call an Uber or phone a friend. It was late, so calling a family member was out of the question unless it was a real emergency. My parents would freak out if the phone rang after nine at night. Nobody calls with good news after nine p.m.

I could call Patty, but considering she was eight months pregnant and on maternity leave, she probably wouldn't appreciate the late-night call. That left Tate. I knew she'd jump on her bike and come get me, but the thought of being a damsel in distress rubbed me the wrong way. I didn't need rescuing. Just because I wasn't very tall or muscular didn't mean I couldn't take care of myself. I called an Uber.

Fifteen minutes later, the driver pulled up next to my car in the probation department parking lot. As I got out of the car, I noticed a piece of paper on my windshield. Someone had written in red pen: "I'm coming for you, bitch. You can run, but you can't hide." It had to be Max.

My heart pounded in my chest. *What the fuck?* I quickly scanned my surroundings. I was completely alone. But just in case I wasn't, I took out my weapon with one hand, unlocked and opened the car door with the other. I looked around again, climbed in, locked the door, and holstered my gun. I reread the note as I started the car, then called Tate. A part of me was mad at myself for needing help, but the other part, the less stubborn part, knew it was a good call. Maybe I didn't need rescuing, but I did need a cop.

The phone rang once, and Tate picked up. "Are you done with your stakeout?"

"How did you know I was on a stakeout?" Tate had eyes everywhere. It was hard to do anything without her knowing about it.

"Cup and Skylar drove by earlier looking for Pinky and saw you in the car with McCarthy." She chuckled. "Stan must be really pissed at you if he sent you out with him."

I took a deep breath and let it out slowly. "Yeah, he's still pissed, and I'm being punished."

"Did he have a burrito for lunch?" She laughed out loud.

"Worse, an egg salad sandwich. The car smelled bad for an hour. The burrito was for dinner."

"Yikes. That's bad."

"Yeah, it was. But that's not why I'm calling." I pulled my car out of the parking lot and turned toward home. "When I got back to my car, there was a note on the windshield."

"Love note?"

I couldn't tell if she was worried someone else might be interested in me or trying to be funny.

"No. Another threat. He said he's coming for me."

I could hear Tate moving things around. "Are you on your way home?"

"Yes, I just pulled out of the parking lot."

"Okay. Don't go into your apartment until I get there. Wait in the car," she said. "You have your weapon with you, don't you?"

"Of course."

"Okay, keep it out and ready."

"Okay."

"And, Riley?"

"What?"

"Don't accidentally shoot me when I get there."

"Don't even joke about things like that. It's not funny."

"Okay, babe, I'll be right there."

Tate and I lived three blocks apart, so I knew she'd probably beat me there. Sure enough, when I pulled into the driveway, her motorcycle was parked at the bottom of the stairs. The lights were out at Mike's, and I'd forgotten to leave my porchlight on when I'd left this morning, so it was dark. Max could be hiding anywhere.

I'd never given Tate a key to my apartment. It seemed like too big of a commitment, and I didn't like the idea of her being there when I wasn't expecting her. Other than your parents, giving someone a key to your home says a lot of things about the relationship. And I hadn't been ready to say those things. And since the plan was still to apply to the FBI and move to Quantico in the near future...okay, sometime in the future, saying those things seemed like a bad idea.

Tate held a flashlight in one hand and her weapon—pointed at the ground—in the other. I left my gun in its holster on my hip to be safe. Before I climbed out of the car, I grabbed a small flashlight from the glove compartment and met Tate at the bottom of the staircase.

"You couldn't have left a light on?" she asked.

I frowned. "I left at seven this morning. I didn't know I'd be on a stakeout half the night."

"Okay. Let's look around before we go upstairs."

Tate led the way around the exterior of the garage that my apartment was built over. Mike was a neat freak. The bushes had been trimmed recently, and none were big enough for a person to hide behind. When we got back to the staircase, Tate went up first, pointing her flashlight up the stairs at the door. I focused my light behind us, making sure we weren't being followed. At the top of the twelve stairs, Tate stopped and checked around the screen door's frame.

"I don't see any sign that it's been tampered with." She pulled the screen door open. Other than a loud squeak, nothing else happened. She ran the flashlight beam around the edges of the wooden front door. "I don't see anything here either. Go ahead and open it."

I gently slid the key into the lock and turned, then pushed open the door. I reached in and flipped the switch, and light filled the room. I promised myself tomorrow I'd buy a timer for the lamp and set it to come on at dusk.

Tate walked into the living room and looked behind the couch. There wasn't any place else to hide. We went into the kitchen and looked around. All of the cabinets were too small for anyone other than a toddler to hide in, so we proceeded to the bathroom. After pulling back the shower curtain to find an empty bathtub, we moved on to the bedroom. Tate made her way to the closet while I looked under the bed. I knew there was so much junk crammed under there a burglar would have an easier time squeezing into a kitchen cabinet than under there. Tate turned from the closet, holstered her gun, and put her flashlight in her back pocket. "It's clear."

"I could use a beer. How about you?"

"Yeah, a beer would be good."

"There's still some Chinese, want me to heat it up?"

Tate collapsed on a kitchen chair. "Sure." She reached out for the beer. "You're awfully chill about all this."

I closed my eyes, took a deep breath, held it to a count of ten, and let it out. I opened my eyes and looked at her. "As I see it, I have two choices. One, I can fall apart and act like a stereotypical female that can't handle her own shit. Or two, I can suck it up and trust that you will find Max before he burns down my apartment with me in it." I guzzled half the beer.

"No pressure at all, Riley."

"Oh, I almost forgot. I saw Pinky in front of my apartment twice last night. She waved to me, then moseyed off down the street. Like she was out for a stroll."

Tate raised her beer halfway to her mouth and stopped. "What the hell was she up to?" She lifted the beer to her lips.

"Then she called this morning on my personal phone."

Tate almost spit out the beer, but she slapped a napkin to her mouth. "She has your phone number?"

"She took my business card out of her mother's purse. It was written on the back."

"You gave her mother your phone number?"

"It was years ago when Pinky was a teen and had run away from home."

Tate leaned her head to the side and looked at me like I was crazy.

"What can I say? I was a new PO and wanted to save the world."

"And it's come back to bite you in the butt." She lifted the bottle to her mouth again.

"She wanted to talk to you, actually."

"Why? She can turn herself in to you. What does she need me for?"

"She wants to make a deal."

"What kind?"

"She'll give you information about Lester Knight and a big drug deal in exchange for letting her go."

"There are at least two warrants out for her. I can't ignore them." I could see the wheels spinning in her head.

"What are you thinking?"

"Pinky might make a good CI, if I can convince my lieutenant, and we can get the DA to make her a deal on the theft charges."

"If she'll take the deal, and if she'll agree to be your snitch. Those are big ifs."

"Snitch is such an ugly word. I prefer confidential informant."

"Tomato, tamoto." I shrugged. "It's all the same thing."

"Okay, I'll talk with her. Who knows, maybe we can work something out?"

"I'll heat up the leftovers."

She finished her beer in two long swallows and stood. She took my hand and pulled me to my feet. Her face was inches from mine, and her icy blue eyes laser focused. The scent of her citrus and musk cologne made me giddy. She raised her hand and cupped my cheek. "Forget the leftovers."

I smiled and raised an eyebrow. "Not hungry?"

One side of her mouth raised in a slight grin. "Not for Chinese." She leaned in and captured my mouth with hers, her tongue urgent to find mine. She pulled away. "Bedroom, now."

CHAPTER THIRTEEN

When I woke up the next morning, Tate was gone again. She called a few hours later. She'd met with her lieutenant and been given the go-ahead to recruit Pinky as her confidential informant. Now she was on her way to meet with the assistant deputy district attorney to convince her to offer Pinky a plea deal in exchange for information on Lester Knight and his drug operation.

"Can you text me her number?" She sounded distracted.

"I don't have it. The number is always blocked when she calls. I'll send you her mother's and girlfriend's numbers. I'm pretty sure she's in regular contact with them. At least with Trixie."

"Is that her girlfriend?"

"Yes. Her last name is Adams."

"Okay, I gotta go. I'll call you later."

I pulled up the contact list and sent Pinky's mother and girlfriend's numbers to Tate. Hopefully, the district attorney's office would agree to offer Pinky a deal. She was a small fish. Lester Knight, on the other hand, was a very big fish.

I didn't hear from Tate until ten that night. She sounded exhausted. The deputy district attorney had agreed to offer Pinky a deal if she cooperated with the police. Tate had contacted Pinky through her girlfriend, and she'd agreed to the terms. A meeting with the narcotics unit was set up for the following morning.

First thing Wednesday morning, I went looking for Stan to update him on the Pinky situation. I found him in the break room, a powdered donut in his hand, powder on his chin, and the front of his navy-blue dress shirt.

"What now, Reynolds?" he asked, taking another bite of the donut.

"The district attorney's office made a deal with Pinky Higgins."

His eyebrows scrunched together, and wrinkles appeared on his forehead. "What kind of deal?"

"She's going to give them information to take down Lester Knight, and in return, she gets probation for stealing the car and stays out of prison." I didn't think telling him Pinky would become a confidential informant for Tate necessary.

"Shit. I don't like it, but there's nothing we can do about it." He shoved the rest of the donut in his mouth.

I shook my head, trying to give the impression that I didn't like it either. "Well, on the upside, they'll get Lester Knight off the street."

He huffed. "Won't matter. Some other lowlife will take his place before he's even had a bail hearing."

I exhaled. "You're probably right. I'll be in my office if you need me." I hurried down the hall before he thought of some menial tasks to saddle me with just because he could.

By two o'clock, I'd reviewed three or four dozen warrant files, drunk too many cups of bad coffee, and hadn't had anything to eat. I stood, stretched, and in my head, ran through a list of places to get a quick bite. Deciding on the sandwich place a few blocks from the office, I grabbed my jacket and started to walk out the door when the phone rang. I answered it, hoping it was Tate or Pinky with an update. But it wasn't. Detective Juan Lopez from the SLO County Sheriff's narcotics unit wanted my help. His informant spilled the beans on my probationer Monica Stevens. Apparently, she was transporting cocaine for her boyfriend and consuming some of the product. It wasn't unusual for a probationer to use drugs, but Monica was seven months pregnant. The detective asked if I would test her. If she was positive, maybe he could get her to flip on her boyfriend in exchange for a recommendation that she go to rehab rather than prison. She already had two possession charges, so prison was a real possibility. She'd be smart to take the deal.

I called Monica to report in at three. She arrived thirty minutes late. When I told her I needed a urine sample, she swore she couldn't go. I've never been pregnant and can say with one hundred percent certainty that I never will be, but I do know how often a pregnant woman has to pee. Patty has three kids and was about to deliver the fourth, and she had to pee every twenty minutes. So, when Monica said she couldn't go, I was doubtful but willing to play along. I had been saving 32 oz cups from 7-Eleven for just such occasions.

I filled the cup to the top with water and handed it to her, then showed her to a comfy chair outside my office. At four o'clock, I checked on her. The cup was empty, but she claimed she still couldn't go. I shrugged, took the cup, refilled it, and handed it back to her. At four-thirty, I checked on her again. The cup was empty, but she again claimed she couldn't go. This time, however, her legs were crossed. I didn't think she could hold out much longer. I refilled the cup, returned it to her, and said, "Don't worry about the time. My boss is fine with overtime for special cases." I smiled. I could tell she was grinding her teeth, trying to hold it in. It wouldn't be long now.

While I waited, I called Tate. She answered on the first ring.

"Hi, babe. Sorry I haven't called."

"No problem. I was just checking in." Out of the corner of my eye, I saw Monica squirm in the chair outside my office. "I only have a few minutes. How did it go?"

"It's all set up. The bust is Sunday night. That's about all I can say for now."

"I understand," I said, disappointed I wasn't getting any details. "How did P—"

"I have to go!" Monica screamed as she ran into my office.

"The bathroom's down the hall." I pointed. "Tate, I have to go. I'll call you later." I hung up before she could say goodbye and hurried after Monica.

Two steps into the restroom, she screamed, "Fuck!" The front of her sweatpants turned dark gray all the way down her legs, and 96 ounces of water puddled on the floor. She looked at me, her face beet red.

I stepped around the mess and handed her the container. "You better have a little left, or you aren't going anywhere."

Luckily, she did have an ounce left. After she handed it back to me, I inserted a test strip which instantly turned blue, showing the presence of cocaine. I showed it to her and shook my head. "You know what this means, right?"

She began to cry. Great racking sobs, and massive tears poured down her face as she pulled her soaking-wet sweatpants up. "Please don't take me to jail," she wailed. "Please, please, please don't take me to jail." She sobbed and screamed at the same time.

Her hysterics got Stan's attention, and he stepped out of his office, Snickers bar in hand. "Reynolds, what the hell is going on?"

"She's seven months pregnant and tested positive for cocaine."

He stared at Monica, his eyes narrowed. "Make sure you get her cleared at the hospital before she goes to jail." He took a bite of the candy bar, stepped back into his office, and closed the door.

It was just my luck, there was a full moon, and the hospital was a zoo. It took two hours to get her cleared, then another hour to get her booked at the jail. I was a zombie when I walked into my apartment at nine and went straight to the shower and to bed. It's a glamorous life, being a probation officer.

CHAPTER FOURTEEN

I walked into Department 12 of the superior court for Manny Martinez's detention hearing at nine Thursday morning. A few people sat in the gallery, and half a dozen defendants sat in the jury box. I've always thought it strange that they put those accused of a crime in the jury box, where jurors would sit to judge those charged with crimes a few hours later. The bailiff called the room to order, and everyone stood.

"…The honorable Melinda F. Bookings presiding."

The judge took her seat behind the bench, which was a silly name for the oversize, padded chair that sat three feet off the floor so the judge could look down at her minions. I couldn't help but smile, remembering what Bud said about the courthouse's pet name for her.

"You may be seated," the bailiff said then returned to his seat near the jury box. The court clerk called Manny's case. Judge Bookings glanced around the courtroom and set her gaze on Manny, then his court-appointed lawyer, Sam Smith.

"Mr. Martinez, you are here regarding a violation of probation for failing to report to your probation officer. How do you plead?"

Manny's lawyer stood. "My client pleads not guilty, Your honor. Mr. Martinez missed his appointment with the probation officer because he was in the hospital for three days due to a severe case of food poisoning."

The judge raised an eyebrow. "Give me a minute to review the file."

The lawyer smiled and winked at Manny as the judge read the paperwork. After a few minutes, she looked up with a serious expression and addressed Manny's lawyer again.

"Mr. Smith, it says here your client's appointment with his probation officer was on February 5th, 2021. So, he claims he was in the hospital on that date?"

"Yes, Your Honor, that is correct."

I had to suppress a laugh. Judge Bookings had set a trap, and the smug lawyer was too full of himself to see what was coming.

"Mr. Smith, your client was detained by Officer Reynolds on September 8th, 2022, correct?" The smile on her lips did not reach her eyes.

The lawyer paused. "Yes, Your Honor. It is."

"So, if your client was in the hospital on the day of his probation appointment a year and a half ago, why didn't he call and reschedule it when he was released?"

I had to suppress a chuckle as the lawyer shifted his feet nervously. "Your Honor, may I have a moment to confer with my client?"

"You have two minutes, Mr. Smith. I do not have all day."

Smith turned to Manny and spoke in a low voice. The two of them had a brief discussion, then the lawyer turned back to Judge Bookings.

"Your Honor, my client claims he forgot. It was an innocent oversight."

I had to lean forward and cover my mouth with my hand. It was all I could do not to laugh.

The judge narrowed her eyes and glared at the lawyer. He wasn't looking quite so smug now. "Mr. Smith, did your client innocently forget that he was on probation for the past year and a half?"

"Uh—"

"Never mind, Mr. Smith." She looked at me in the front of the gallery. "Officer Reynolds, do you have a recommendation on the defendant's release?"

I was enjoying the show so much she'd caught me off guard. I probably had that deer-in-the-headlights look on my face. I rose to my feet. "Um, Your Honor, the fact that Mr. Martinez hasn't contacted the probation department for a year and a half says it all, I think. I would not recommend he be released."

"I agree." She turned her attention on Manny. "Mr. Martinez, you are detained in the county jail until your revocation hearing. I'm setting that for one month from today."

Smith wasn't going to let it go. "Your Honor, my client is—"

The judge held up her hand. "Mr. Smith, we are done here. Clerk, please call the next case." She placed Manny's file to the side and picked up the next one on her pile.

Smith slumped in his chair like a deflated balloon as the bailiff escorted Manny out of the courtroom. I couldn't help but smile. The party was over. I only hoped that Manny didn't end up holding a grudge like Max had.

As I stood to leave, the petite blond deputy district attorney turned around. She smiled at me and winked, then, without saying a word, turned back around as the next case was called.

As I walked up the aisle to the big oak doors, I wondered why she'd winked at me. Was she flirting with me? That kind of thing didn't happen to me. Women flirted with Tate all the time, but not with me. It made me feel strange, but I liked it.

As I reached to open the door, someone pushed from the other side, almost hitting me in the face. I froze, startled. It was Michelle, my almost ex-fiancée. It had been nearly four years since I'd seen her. She looked as surprised to see me as I did her.

"What are you doing here?" My heart pounded in my ears. What was she doing here? This was where I lived. How dare she trespass into my life after what she'd done.

"I could ask you the same thing," she said.

"I work here." I opened my jacket so she could see my probation badge.

"So do I." The smile on her lips didn't reach her eyes.

There was a tap on my shoulder. The bailiff had walked up behind me, and he wasn't smiling. "Ladies, take it outside."

Michelle and I both whispered our apologies and stepped out into the hall.

I kept my voice low and tried to remain professional. We were in a courthouse, after all. "What do you mean you *work* here?" I knew almost everyone who worked in the building. Michelle was not one of those people. My mind spun in confusion. "What do you mean?" I asked, my voice barely above a whisper.

"I was hired by a law firm here in town."

What the fuck? "You're a lawyer?"

"I finished law school in May. I still have to pass the bar."

I could feel a headache coming on. "Please don't tell me you moved here."

"We did. Two months ago."

"We?"

"Brenda and I. We're married."

Of course, she would marry the woman she'd cheated on me with.

"You couldn't have gotten a job anywhere else? You knew I was from here."

"First of all, I didn't know you'd moved back here. And Smith, Smith, and Aldridge is an all-female law firm. That appealed to me."

It took everything I had to remain calm. I glared at her. "Just fucking perfect." I turned and walked away, almost running into Cup and Skyler.

"Hey, what's the hurry?" Skyler asked.

"Sorry, I'm late for court," I lied and hurried off. The walls felt like they were closing in. I needed fresh air.

I exited the courthouse into the sunlight and headed to my car. I took a deep breath, counted to ten, and slowly exhaled. As

I stepped into the street, a familiar figure called out my name. It was Tate. The mischievous grin on her face set off butterflies, replacing the churning acid in my stomach.

When she got close, she snapped her fingers in front of my face. I was still standing in the middle of the street. "Riley, you're holding up traffic."

I shook myself and walked to the curb. "What are you doing here?"

"I have to testify in Judge Bookings's court at eleven." She frowned. "What's wrong?"

I paused and took a deep breath. "I ran into Michelle in the courthouse this morning."

"Michelle, your ex?"

I nodded. "She was hired at a law firm in town."

"She moved here?"

"She and Brenda." I looked up at the cloudless blue sky. "Can you believe it?"

Tate placed her hand on my cheek. "I have to get to court. Will you be okay?"

I nodded.

"Okay, I'll call you later." She gave me a quick hug and then headed into the building.

I made my way to my car and headed for the office. The minute I walked in, Stan appeared with a stack of warrant files and unceremoniously dumped them on my desk. "Find them sooner rather than later," he grumbled and walked away without another word.

I counted twelve files. At least this would keep me busy and my mind off my ex's surprise appearance today. I let out a sigh and started to sift through the files. The third one I opened was a guy by the name of Eddie Easter, a three-time offender. He had a history of drug possession and one count of assault, the victim had been his girlfriend. I located his address in the file, grabbed my keys, and headed out. Hopefully, going after him would take my mind off my crappy morning.

I drove to Easter's last known address: a rundown trailer park in Atascadero, a small town just north of SLO. I pulled up in front of his trailer. A faded yellow rust bucket, probably held together with baling wire and duct tape was parked in the driveway. Cardboard covered the windows of the single wide trailer. I knocked on the door several times. I didn't hear anything inside—no voices, no TV or radio playing, and no one came to the door.

As I walked back to my car, I noticed an elderly woman across the street sitting in a rocking chair, watching me from the porch of her trailer. Judging by the leathery skin on her face and hands, she looked to be at least a hundred years old. She motioned me over.

"You looking for that piece of shit Eddie Easter?" Apparently, she wasn't one to hold back her opinions.

"Yes, ma'am. Have you seen him?"

She waved a hand in the direction of a trailer at the far end of the park. "He moved a while ago. He lives over there now, the baby-shit green one." She had the rusty voice of someone who'd been smoking for more years than I'd been alive. "But he ain't there. He left with that floozy of his about an hour ago. Probably to get himself more drugs."

"You think he's using drugs?"

Before she answered, she began coughing, hacking up phlegm. She pulled a hanky from the ruffled end of her sleeve and spit into it. I swallowed hard to keep from gagging, thankful I hadn't eaten lunch yet.

She wiped her mouth and shoved the hanky back up her sleeve. "He's doing more than using them. Cars coming and going from his place at all hours of the night. You'd think it was McDonald's. A body can't get a good night's sleep with the traffic through here."

"So you think he's selling them?"

"I don't know why so many people would be parading through here all hours of the night. Do you?"

"No, can't say that I do, but I'll see what I can do about it." I started down the steps, then turned back. "I'd appreciate it if you didn't tell him I was looking for him."

"It'll be our little secret." She smiled and resumed her rocking.

I turned to leave, but then something else occurred to me. "Do you know who the floozy is?"

The woman chuckled. "When they're fighting, he calls her bitch. But I think her name's Alice. I've been told she's a cocktail waitress at the strip club down the street. I'll bet you dollars to donuts she does more than serve cocktails."

I smiled. "I'll bet you're right."

I noted the address of Easter's trailer and got back in my car. On my way back to the office, I stopped at In-N-Out Burger and got a Double-Double with fries and a Diet Coke. I like to cut calories where I can. I pulled into a space in the parking lot and ate in the car.

My mind wandered to the courtroom and literally running into Michelle. It had been four years since I'd caught her cheating on me, but it felt like only yesterday. I thought I'd let it go, but apparently, I was still angry. Was it any wonder I had trust issues?

I finished the last of my fries and tossed the remains into the trash on my way out of the lot. When I got back to the office, I called the Atascadero Police Department. It's a small department without a dedicated narcotics unit, so I asked for the desk sergeant. I was transferred to Sergeant Forman. I explained who I was and gave him the information on Easter, the outstanding warrant, and that I suspected he was dealing drugs from his trailer. The sergeant thanked me for the tip and said they'd take care of it.

One down, eleven to go.

CHAPTER FIFTEEN

At three a.m. the phone rang, interrupting my hot, steamy sex dream with Cate Blanchett. Cate was wearing the black tux she wore in the movie *Tor*, and I was wearing...well, nothing. I grabbed the phone and punched the green button.

"What?" I answered, annoyed.

"Your aunt is missing." My father sounded frantic.

It took me a second to transition from Cate's face between my legs and my father's worried voice, not an easy thing to do. "Dad?"

"Riley, your aunt is missing. She went out with a friend and said she'd be back early." I pictured my dad pacing back and forth across the kitchen in his pajamas. I also knew that "early" was a malleable term to my aunt. For her, early could mean two or three in the morning. I also knew she'd probably been at the Friday night poker game in the back room of McGee's Pub.

"Did you try calling her?"

"Of course I did. She's not answering."

"Did she say where she was going?"

"I don't know. A movie, maybe?"

"Who was she with?" I crawled out of bed.

"I'm not sure, someone picked her up, but they didn't come in the house."

"Okay, Dad. I might know where she is." I turned on the bedside lamp.

"Where?"

"There's a secret Friday night poker game. She's probably there."

"Riley, it's three o'clock in the morning!"

I slipped out of my pajama bottoms and pulled on a pair of jeans. "I know, Dad," I said as I traded the Indigo Girls T-shirt I'd worn to bed for a bra and sweatshirt. "I'll drive down there and see if it's still going on."

"I can't believe she'd worry us like this. She's fifty years old. She should know better. If she's going to act like a teenager, we're going to have to put some rules in place."

That almost made me laugh. Giving Aunt Liz rules to follow would be like asking water to run uphill. I slipped into my tennis shoes that I'd taken off the night before without untying. "Okay, Dad. I'll call you as soon as I know something." I grabbed my keys and pepper spray from the drawer. I'd never gotten around to getting a concealed weapon permit so legally I was only allowed to carry my firearm when working. As I headed down the stairs, I called Tate. She was used to getting calls from work in the middle of the night. She answered on the first ring.

"What's wrong?" She sounded wide awake.

"Sorry if I woke you. Aunt Liz didn't come home after the poker game. My dad is freaking out."

"Those games end by midnight. It's kind of an unwritten rule."

"I know. I'm on my way there now. Can you meet me?" I asked as I started my car and put it in reverse.

"I'm walking out the door," she said and hung up.

Driving down Monterey Street at 3:15 in the morning was eerie. It was deserted, even the homeless were tucked in somewhere. When I turned the corner at Osos, several expensive cars were parked on the street on either side of the alley behind McGee's. All had yellow parking tickets on the windshields. I drove down the alley with a bad feeling in the pit of my stomach. I breathed a sigh of relief when I saw Tate's motorcycle, and stopped behind it. The lights were on inside the pub, and Tate was trying the back door.

She walked up as I got out of the car. "It's locked. I pounded on it, but no one came. I don't hear anything inside either."

"Crap. There are cars on the street, and they've been ticketed. Even if the game went late, someone would feed the meters."

Tate nodded. "I don't like it, Riley. Something's not right."

It was absolutely quiet. The only sound was the rattle of a loose screen in the early-morning breeze.

"Riley?" She looked up and down the alley. "Do you smell smoke?"

I froze and concentrated on my breathing and the smell in the air. At first, the only thing I noticed was the odor of rotting food coming from a nearby dumpster. Then I smelled it, the faint scent of woodsmoke. "Fuck! Where's it coming from?" My head swiveled around, looking everywhere. Then I saw it, grayish smoke slowly creeping from under the door Tate had just found locked. "Oh my God, Tate, it's in the building."

"Shit! Riley, call 911." She ran to the trunk of my car. "And pop your trunk."

I pressed the button on my key as I dialed 911. Tate took out the tire iron, ran to the window, smashed it, and then scraped around the edges, clearing away shards of glass. "Riley, give me a boost!"

I held the phone between my ear and shoulder and laced my fingers together to make a cradle for her to step in. She grabbed the windowsill, muscled her upper body up, and swung one leg and then the other inside. Then she disappeared inside the building. Just as I finished with 911, the door opened. Tate crouched inside, her shirt pulled up to just below her eyes, and smoke rose around her.

"Pull your shirt over your nose and stay as low as you can!"

I did as she said, and we made our way, bent at the knees in a squat. Not surprising, Tate, ever the Girl Scout, had a flashlight, so we could see several feet ahead. We'd only taken a few steps when we saw them—tied to chairs, silver duct tape over their mouths, and all four unconscious.

Tate jumped into action, pulled a folding knife out of her pocket, and cut the zip ties holding Aunt Liz to the chair. "Grab her under the arms and drag her out!" she yelled as she moved to the next person. Judge Bookings sat tied to the chair, her head sagging forward.

I ran behind my aunt, slid my arms under her armpits, and pulled with every ounce of strength I had. Luckily, Aunt Liz was a petite woman and didn't weigh much. I could hear sirens not far away as I moved backward toward the exit, dragging her with me.

Just as we made it to the alley, a fire truck arrived. Firefighters jumped out and started grabbing equipment and hoses as an ambulance pulled up behind them. Tate was just coming out, dragging the judge.

"There's two more inside!" I yelled to the first firefighter to reach me. She nodded and started ordering other firefighters into action.

I laid Aunt Liz on the ground as a paramedic ran up and kneeled across from me.

"She's breathing," I said, coughing.

"Go to the ambulance and get yourself checked out," she said.

I shook my head. I wasn't going to leave Aunt Liz's side until they loaded her onto a gurney and placed an oxygen mask on her face. I was so worried about my aunt that I hadn't noticed Tate standing beside me, covered in black soot.

"Come on, Riley, she's in good hands." Tate put an arm around my shoulder and led me to one of the other ambulances.

"I'm okay," I insisted. "Will you drive my car to the hospital? I'll go in the ambulance with Aunt Liz."

"Sure." She hugged me and placed a kiss on the side of my head. "She'll be okay."

I swallowed a sob. Tears welled in my eyes. "I have to call my parents," I said, wiping my face.

"Okay, I'll meet you there." She helped me into the back of the ambulance.

Before she closed the doors, I stopped her. "Tate, is it Max? Did he do this?" I wanted her to tell me no, that it was a robbery and not connected to Max.

"I don't know, Riley. It might be."

I nodded. I knew it was. My eyes locked on hers until the ambulance doors closed. I took out my phone and called my parents. Luckily the siren wasn't blaring because that would freak them out and send them over the edge.

My dad answered before the end of the first ring. "Riley, did you find her?"

"Yes. We're on our way to Mom's hospital. Meet us there."

"What happened? Is she okay?"

"I don't know. She doesn't appear to be hurt, but she's unconscious. So are the three others that were with her." I looked down at my aunt lying on the gurney. An oxygen mask covered most of her face. A paramedic inserted a needle into her arm, which I assumed would start fluids.

"What the hell was she up to, Riley?" His voice was a cross between frantic and pissed off. I could hear my mother in the background, crying.

"I don't know, Dad," I said, exhausted. "We'll figure it out. For now, meet me at the hospital, okay?"

"We'll be right there," he said, and the line went dead.

The ambulance pulled into the ER sally port, and the doors opened. As I jumped out, I heard a siren not far off and knew more were coming. Tate, driving my car, pulled into a parking space in the first row, got out, and rushed over.

Things moved fast until they didn't. They rushed Aunt Liz and the judge into the ER and directed us to a waiting area. My parents and sister arrived a few minutes later, distraught and shocked at the sight of Tate and me, our clothes disheveled and covered in black soot.

My mother started to cry. "Oh my God, Riley, was there a fire?" She hugged me to her, not caring about the mess I was. "Are you okay?"

I hugged her back, then pulled away. "Yes, there was a fire. And yes, Tate and I are okay." I wiped tears from my face with the back of my hand.

Dad put his arm around my shoulder and handed me his handkerchief.

"Thanks." I wiped the soot from my face.

"What happened, Riley?" Dad asked. "How bad is Liz?"

"She was unconscious when we found her but didn't appear to be injured."

Tate cleared her throat. "Riley, can I talk to you for a minute?" She pulled me aside and asked me not to tell them about how we found them, that it was a crime scene, and telling them could compromise the investigation.

"Tate, he almost killed my aunt." Tears streamed down my face again. I could smell the smoke on my clothes, making my stomach turn.

She wrapped her arms around me and held me tight. "It'll be okay," she whispered in my ear. "We'll find him."

I almost forgot about everyone else until a doctor entered the waiting room and asked for Elizabeth O'Neal's family. My mom and dad rushed over. I reluctantly let go of Tate and joined them.

"She's my sister," my father told the doctor.

The doctor motioned for us to follow him through the door. Once assembled on the other side, he turned to my father. "Mrs. O'Neal is being treated for mild smoke inhalation. She doesn't have any burns or other injuries that we can find."

"Is she awake?" my mother asked.

He shook his head. "Not fully. And that's concerning. There doesn't appear to be a head injury. I believe she may have been drugged. I've ordered blood tests to determine what it might be."

"Can I see her?" My father's eyes filled with tears.

"Yes, one at a time for a few minutes. Try talking to her, see if she'll come around. But don't push it."

My father wiped away a tear that had escaped down his cheek. "Understood."

"I'll show you to her room," he said. "The rest of you can go back to the waiting room."

Tate stepped forward and took out her badge. "I'm the detective on the case. Can I see Judge Bookings?"

The doctor looked at Tate from head to toe and shook his head. "You need to get checked out and cleaned up first." Then he looked at me. "You too. Follow me, I'll get someone to see you. Then go home and clean up."

Tate didn't look happy, but she didn't argue.

The doctor took us to a small room at the far end of the ER. I sat on the bed, and Tate took a seat on a padded chair. A nurse appeared and put oxygen masks on our faces, pinched a plastic monitor to the index fingers on our right hands, then took each of our blood pressures. When she was done, she removed the monitors from our fingers, said someone would be with us shortly, then left the room. I laid back on the bed, and Tate slumped in the chair. It didn't look comfortable, but within a minute, she was asleep. I must have drifted off too. The sound of the door opening jolted me awake. The gorgeous, redheaded doctor with the steel-blue eyes that had treated Bud walked in.

She looked at Tate like a lioness looks at a gazelle. "Well, if it isn't Detective Walker. Fancy meeting you here."

Apparently, she and Tate knew each other. I immediately despised her.

Tate pulled down the oxygen mask and gave her a small smile. "Hi, Dominique. How are you?"

"Better than you, it looks like," she said, then gave me a smile that didn't quite reach her eyes. "You were here a few days ago, weren't you?"

She made me feel like a bug under a microscope. I pulled off the mask. "Yes. My partner had a broken wrist. I'm Riley Reynolds."

She looked from me to Tate, then back at me, assessing the situation. "All right, let's get the two of you checked out." She took the stethoscope from around her neck, placed it on my chest, and asked me to take a deep breath. "From what I understand, the two of you played superhero this morning and dragged two people out of a burning building? Is that correct?"

"It sounds much more exciting than it was," Tate said.

"If I remember correctly, Ms. Reynolds, you are not a police officer." She moved the stethoscope to my back and told me to take a deep breath.

"No. Probation officer."

She removed the stethoscope and asked me to open my mouth wide. She placed a tongue depressor in my mouth and told me to say, "aah." I followed her instructions.

"I didn't think probation officers were first responders," she said as she typed something into her tiny laptop.

"We aren't. I wasn't there as a probation officer. My aunt didn't come home last night, and my father was worried. I asked Tate to help me look for her. We were just in the right place at the right time."

She moved to stand in front of Tate. "I'll say." She placed the stethoscope on Tate's chest and asked her to take a deep breath, then moved it to Tate's back and asked the same thing. If you ask me, she leaned in a little more than necessary, her boob rubbing against Tate's shoulder. Tate seemed oblivious, though.

After looking in Tate's throat, she typed on her little laptop again, then turned back to us. "I haven't heard either of you cough, so that's good. I didn't detect any shortness of breath. Your oximeter readings and blood pressure are within normal ranges. Do either of you have a headache?"

We both shook our heads.

"Good," she said. "Dizziness?"

We shook our heads again.

"Good. That could indicate carbon monoxide poisoning." She typed into the laptop again and then looked up. "However, it can take twenty-four to forty-eight hours for some of the symptoms to appear. So, if any of them do, come back here immediately. Smoke inhalation can have serious complications. I'll also order some blood tests to check for heavy metals or other toxic substances that you might have inhaled." She typed again on the laptop and then looked up. "I would advise you to remember that you're not actually superheroes, and you should leave running into burning buildings to firefighters who are trained for that sort of thing."

Tate chuckled. "Thanks, Dominique. We'll keep that in mind next time."

She smiled and picked up her laptop. "You do that." She looked at me. "Ms. Reynolds, good to see you again. But I hope I don't see either of you back in my ER as patients anytime soon." She opened the door then turned back. "A nurse will be right in to get that blood, then you can get cleaned up." Without another word, she was gone.

I looked at Tate, my right eyebrow raised. "You know her?" Jealousy crept up my back. I shouldn't be jealous. I was the one who didn't want a commitment, but I didn't like that another woman might be interested in Tate either.

Tate shrugged. "Over the years, I've spent a lot of time in the ER. You get to know people."

"She—"

A male nurse with a tray of syringes and glass tubes walked in. He looked at us and made a tsking sound with his tongue. He reached into a drawer under the bed and pulled out two paper gowns. "You'll both need to take those tops off, and I'll give you some antiseptic wipes to clean off whichever arm you want me to use for the blood draw." He handed us each a gown. "I'll be right back."

Tate and I pulled our jackets and T-shirts off and tossed them aside. The thought of putting them back on turned my stomach. "So, about the doctor—" I began but the door opened, interrupting me again.

The nurse held green scrubs in his hands. "I asked Doctor Ross if we could loan you something to wear home, and she said yes, as long as you bring them back clean." He set them on the end of the bed. "And here's two plastic bags to put your clothes in." He laid the bags on top of the scrubs. "Now, let's get that blood and get the two of you out of here. You're really stinking up the place," he chuckled.

Twenty minutes later, we returned to the waiting room, dressed in green scrubs, our faces washed, and carrying our sooty, smelly clothes in plastic bags. My parents were still there, each holding a cup of coffee, my sister had gone home.

"How's Aunt Liz?" I asked, hugging my father and then my mother.

"She's awake but groggy," he said. "They're going to keep her for a few days."

"What did they say about smoke inhalation?" I asked.

"They'll know more when she's fully awake and the blood tests come back." He took a sip of his coffee. "I'm going to stay here. Would you give your mom a ride home?"

"Sure." I put my arm around my mom, then turned to Tate. "Do you want me to take you to get your motorcycle?"

"Thanks, but I'm going to stick around and see if I can talk to the judge and Liz. I'll find someone to give me a ride later."

"Okay. Will you come by later?"

"After I go home and clean up." She pulled me to her. "We'll get him, Riley. I promise you, we'll get him."

I didn't say it out loud, but I hoped they stopped him before he killed me.

CHAPTER SIXTEEN

When I dropped Mom off, the sun shone over the Cuesta foothills to the east. When I pulled up in front of my apartment, Mike came out his back door waving his hands.

"Riley! Riley! Are you okay? Is your aunt okay?" He wrapped his arms around me in a hug and then let go.

"How did you know?" I asked, confused.

He smiled. "Nurse Timmy called."

"Nurse Timmy?"

"He took your blood and gave you those horrid clothes to wear." He pointed to the scrubs. "They really should find a better tailor."

"How did the nurse know I knew you?"

"You didn't recognize him? He used to be my cabana boy."

"Cabana boy? I don't understand. You don't have a pool."

"Riley, you don't need a pool to need the services of a cabana boy." He winked.

I burst out laughing. It felt good. "Okay. I see. Kinda like a house boy?"

"Exactly. Now tell me what happened."

"Mike, I really need a shower and coffee. Can I come over later?"

"Of course. I'll make you breakfast."

"Sounds like heaven," I said, starting up the stairs and taking my filthy tennis shoes off at the door. They'd be going in the trash.

Before I headed to the shower, I called Tate to have her bring her bag of clothes over later, and I'd throw them in with mine. No sense in both of us gumming up our washing machines. She didn't pick up, so I left a message.

I brushed my teeth, turned the water in the shower as hot as possible, peeled off the loaner scrubs, and stepped in.

As I dried off, my phone rang. I wrapped a towel around myself and walked into the kitchen. It had stopped ringing and gone to voice mail. I tapped the little icon to find it was Tate. She'd be over this evening with her clothes and a pizza. Score! I hoped she remembered to get beer.

I smiled as I went to the bedroom and toweled myself dry. Tate really was the perfect girlfriend. I abruptly looked in the mirror. Wrinkles appeared on my forehead, and my mouth scrunched to one side. What was happening? Was I in love? I mean, I loved Tate, and our chemistry was off the charts. But was I *in love* with her? Oh my God! I think I was. How the fuck did I let that happen? And, more importantly, what the hell was I going to do about it?

I finished drying off and pulled on a pair of gray sweats emblazoned with the CSU FRESNO logo down the leg and a Kaki King T-shirt. Tate and I had seen her a few years ago when she'd performed at the Fremont Theater on Monterey Street. I slipped into flip-flops and headed over to Mike's to see what he'd cooked for breakfast. The back door was open. Apparently, he wasn't keeping things locked up like I'd asked.

I was greeted by the smell of vanilla and blueberries, and my stomach growled. Mike stood in front of the stove in a bright red and black kimono, flipping pancakes and singing along to a Barbra Streisand tune from a portable speaker on the counter.

"Good morning," I said, taking a seat at the counter.

"Good morning, dear." He flipped a pancake. "Help yourself to coffee."

I poured myself a cup. "Mike, the door wasn't locked."

He waved a hand. "I knew you'd be right over, so I left it open." He removed several pancakes from the pan, placed them on a plate, and then added a dab of butter.

I blew on my coffee before taking a sip. "You need to keep things locked up until we catch this guy."

Mike placed the plate in front of me. "All right. I will. Now eat my famous blueberry pancakes while they're hot." He handed me a bottle of syrup.

"They smell delicious." The first bite set off flavor fireworks in my mouth. They were divine. "Oh my God, they're so good. How do you do it?" I took another huge bite.

He smiled and wagged a finger at me. "It's a secret. I'll leave it to you in my will."

"You better." I poured a tiny amount of syrup on the remaining pancakes.

He retrieved a carton of orange juice and poured juice into two glasses. "How's your aunt?" He slid one of the glasses over to me.

I frowned. "When I left, they were going to run some tests. She was in and out of consciousness. The doctor thought she and the others may have been drugged." I licked the syrup off my lips and was tempted to lick the plate.

"Drugged?" His forehead wrinkled.

I looked over his shoulder to see if there were any more pancakes to be found. "Maybe GHB. It's the only thing that makes sense."

"Was it a robbery?"

"I don't know. Tate will have some answers when she comes over tonight." I wiped a small amount of purple juice from my plate and licked it off my finger.

Mike shook his head. "Riley, if you want more, just ask."

I picked up my plate and held it out to him. "Please, sir, I want some more," I said in my best cockney orphan voice.

He laughed. "Okay, Oliver, more pancakes coming right up."

Back in my apartment a half hour later, I considered going for a run to burn off the blueberry pancakes. I'd consumed them as if they were the last food on Earth. However, a wave of exhaustion rolled over me and I curled up on the couch with Katherine V. Forrest's latest novel, *Delafield*. It was the series' final book, and it saddened me. I've read the Kate Delafield books since I discovered them in college. Reading the last one was like saying goodbye to an old friend you knew you'd never see again. I had shared them with Tate, who remarked that Katherine must be great at research because she nailed what it was like to be a female detective in a man's world.

Pounding pulled me from a deep sleep. As I jumped up and headed to the door, I glanced at the clock on the kitchen counter—noon. I peered out the peephole, but there wasn't anyone there. I walked back to the couch and looked out the living room window. I didn't see anyone in front of the garage or driveway. I returned to the door and looked out the peephole again; no one was there. What the hell was going on? Did I dream the pounding? I wasn't going to open the door and look out. What if Max was hiding on the stairs? I picked up my phone and called Mike to have him look out his kitchen window and see if anyone was hanging around. He didn't answer and it went to voice mail. I left a message asking him to call me back, and I shoved the phone in my pocket, went back to the couch, picked up *Delafield*, and began reading again.

Two hours later, I closed the book. I was sad that I'd finished, but I felt good that Kate Delafield was in a good place after all her trials and tribulations. I would miss the character, but there were thousands of other lesfic books to explore.

Wondering how my aunt was doing, I called my father. He answered on the first ring.

"Hi, Riley." He sounded upbeat.

"How's she doing, Dad?" I went to the kitchen for some Constant Comet tea. The citrus scent always perked me up.

"She's awake but doesn't remember anything after she arrived at the pub."

"What about smoke inhalation?"

"She's coughing some, and her throat is sore, but she's not dizzy and doesn't have a headache. The doctor said that's a good sign."

"That's good to hear." I turned on my electric kettle and dropped a tea bag in a mug.

"They're going to keep her overnight for observation."

"Should I come down so you can go home for a while?"

"No, your mother's here, so I'll run home and shower. Liz wants a chocolate shake, so I'll pick one up and stay until visiting hours end."

"Okay, I'll see her in the morning."

"I'm sure she'd like that." He paused. "Have you talked to Tate? Have they caught the guy who did this?"

The electric kettle's rumble died, and I poured water into the mug. "I haven't talked to her since we left the hospital this morning. But she'd have let me know if they had." I drizzled honey into the mug and stirred. "She's coming over later to do laundry. I'll know more then."

"Okay. Riley, make sure your doors and windows are locked."

I smiled. "Of course. I'll recheck them all just to be sure. Give Aunt Liz a kiss for me. I'll call you later if I find anything out."

After the call ended, I picked up my mug of tea and returned to the couch, wondering about the pounding on the door. Before I sat down, I looked out the window and surveyed the street. I walked back to the door and looked out the peephole again. No one stood on the other side. Was someone screwing with me or was it a very real dream? As I sat down, my phone rang. It was Mike.

"Hello," I said.

"I saw your message. Is anything wrong?"

"I'm not sure. Are you home?"

"I just walked in. Why?"

"Did you see anyone out front when you got back?"

"No, why?"

"It's probably nothing." I chewed on my bottom lip. "I thought someone pounded on my door, but no one was there when I looked out the peephole."

"That's strange. Hang on, let me look out the kitchen window."

I waited a few seconds as I pictured him walking through the house to the kitchen.

"Riley," he said, his tone uncertain.

"What? Is someone there?"

"No, but there's a box on your doorstep."

Fuck, what now? "Mike, I'm going to hang up and call Tate." I disconnected before he could say anything else and called Tate. As usual, she answered on the first ring.

"Riley, I just got home. Is everything okay? Is your aunt all right?"

"Liz is doing as well as can be expected, and as far as everything being okay, I'm not sure."

"What do you mean?"

"A little while ago, someone pounded on my door. I was sound asleep, so getting to the door took me a little while. No one was there when I looked out the peephole, and I didn't see anyone out front."

"Please tell me you didn't open the door."

"No, I didn't. I called Mike to see if he saw anyone. He wasn't home then, but he just called me back and said there's a box on my porch."

"I'm assuming it isn't an Amazon delivery."

I shook my head even though she couldn't see me. "Nope."

"Shit. Riley do not open the door. Go into the bathroom and get in the bathtub. It's the safest place. I'm calling the bomb squad."

"Seriously? Do you really think that's needed?" I headed to the kitchen to get Randolph. If I was going to shelter in the bathroom, I was taking him with me.

"Riley, it's better to be safe than sorry. Call Mike and tell him to stay in his house and away from the windows. I'll call you back." She disconnected.

I picked up Randolph's bowl and my tea and headed to the bathroom, placing both on the edge of the tub. Then I went into the bedroom and grabbed the pillows. If I was going to spend time in an empty bathtub, I was going to be comfortable. After arranging them in the tub, I climbed in and dialed Mike's number. He answered on the first ring.

"What's going on, Riley?" he asked, his voice urgent.

"Mike, I don't want you to panic, but Tate called the bomb squad to come get the box."

"A bomb?" His voice rose an octave.

"Maybe?" I tried to sound like I wasn't freaking out. "The bomb squad is just a precaution." I took a breath. "Listen, Mike, Tate wants you to stay on the other side of your house, away from the windows."

"Oh my God, Riley. Where are you?" He sounded like he was freaking out.

"In the bathtub," I said, watching Randolph swim around. "Mike, Tate said everything will be okay. We have to trust her. I'll talk to you when it's over, okay?"

"All right. I hope Tate's right."

"Me too, Mike. Me too."

Ten minutes later, sirens screamed in the distance, and my phone rang. Tate's picture filled the screen.

"I hear sirens," I said, forgoing niceties.

"The calvary is on the way," she said, trying to sound light.

"God, I hope this really is a bomb. I don't need the humiliation if it turns out to be a crocheted blanket from my grandmother. I'd never live it down."

"Riley, like I said, it's better to play it safe. Besides, the bomb guys live for this kind of thing."

I sipped my tea, glad I'd brought it with me. "They're all very strange. I'm surprised any of them have a girlfriend."

Tate laughed. "And since when does your grandmother crochet?"

"She doesn't. She's not crafty at all. It was the best I could come up with considering the circumstances." I leaned back against the pillows and tried to make myself comfortable. "This would be much more fun if the tub were filled with hot water and bubbles."

"Yeah, I'm sure it would. Maybe some candles and wine?"

"Definitely. We should do that."

"It'll be the first thing we do after we catch this guy."

"Well, maybe not the first thing."

"No? Is there something you'd rather do first?"

"Oh, yeah. There definitely is." Sirens screamed to a stop out front. "They're here, Tate."

"So am I, babe. We'll have you out of there soon. You and Randolph sit tight."

"Okay," I squeaked out. "Tate…"

"Yeah?"

"You know I love you, right?" I could feel a tear run down my cheek.

"I do. I love you too, Riley. Don't worry, we've got this. These guys are the best in the business."

"Okay."

"I gotta go. Just sit tight."

I didn't have a choice, did I?

I watched Randolph happily swimming around in circles, not a care in the world. If he only knew. I closed my eyes and tried to meditate. I counted to twenty, but I couldn't focus, and I didn't know how to meditate anyway, so I gave up. I thought about calling my parents, then decided there was no need to worry them. I could call Patty and see how she was doing, but again, no need to worry a pregnant woman. Then I wondered how Bud was doing. I hadn't talked to him since he'd decided to take a week off and give his wrist a chance to heal. I kinda liked the guy. If it wasn't for Patty being such a great partner, I wouldn't mind if he stayed in the unit permanently. We could be the queer dynamic duo. He, of course, would be Robin, the Boy Wonder, and I'd be Batwoman. I wonder what Tate would think of me in a skintight black bat suit. I'd have to find one in time for Halloween. Assuming I was still alive for Halloween.

As I let my mind wander, I imagined myself in a black bat suit and a naked Tate slowly peeling it off me. Then the phone rang, throwing cold water on that fantasy. Probably for the best. No use getting all excited when everything around me might literally blow up any second. I looked at the phone, it was Tate.

"Tate?"

"Yeah, babe. The guys are dressed and ready to remove the box. We've evacuated Mike and the nearby houses."

"Great, another reason for the neighbors to hate me."

"Frank is walking up the stairs now." I guess she was going to give me blow-by-blow commentary.

"He's at the top of the stairs and looking at the box. I'm guessing to make sure there's no trip wires."

"Tate, where are you?" I asked, worried that she was too close to the action.

"Don't worry, I'm at least a hundred feet away. I have binoculars." She paused. "He's scanning it now."

"Scanning it?"

"They have a handheld x-ray device. Okay, he's picking up the box and starting back down the stairs."

Well, no loud booms. That was a good sign. I closed my eyes, took a deep breath, and let it out. I had to pee like a big dog. Not good timing. I crossed my legs and squeezed.

"He's at the bottom of the stairs and taking the box to the back of the bomb truck." Her commentary continued. "How are you doing?"

"I have to pee like a racehorse."

She laughed out loud. "Hold on. It should only be a few more minutes."

"What do they do with it?"

"The box?"

"Yes, the box." Seriously? Other than peeing, what else would I care about right now?

"The sergeant just told me the x-ray didn't show any metal inside, so that lessens the chances that it's a bomb. But they'll take it to the gun range and blow it up just to be safe."

I squeezed my legs tighter. After all this, the last thing I needed was to wet myself.

"Okay, Riley, it's secured in the truck. You can get out of the tub."

"Thank the goddess." I climbed out. With one hand, I pulled down my sweatpants and plopped down on the toilet. I held Randolph's bowl steady with the other, keeping him carefree and in a state of fishy ignorance.

Someone started pounding on the front door as I pulled my sweats up. I knew it would be Tate. I returned Randolph to his place on the kitchen counter and went to the door. I barely got it open, and Tate rushed in, wrapping me up in a bear hug so tightly I almost couldn't breathe. I hugged her back, closing my eyes and burying my head into the crook of her neck, taking comfort in her scent.

"I was so scared," she whispered in my ear.

I chuckled. "You and me both." I raised my head to look into her eyes. There were tears in them.

She smiled down at me. "Randolph must have been scared shitless."

"You have no idea. He—"

Her lips were on mine, interrupting some pithy comeback about Randolph being a scaredy cat. I melted into the kiss and hugged her tighter. I briefly flashed to her, peeling the bat suit off me, then someone behind her loudly cleared their throat, and we quickly stepped away from each other. It was Frank, the bomb squad guy, now back in regular clothes.

"Sorry to interrupt, but we're ready to leave," he said. "Tate, I'll call you after we dispose of it."

Tate held out her hand, and he shook it. "Thanks, Frank. I owe you one."

"Naw, just doing my job. Someone will be by later to get your statement, Riley."

"I'll be here," I said.

He gave Tate a small salute. "Have a good rest of your day." He smiled and walked back down the stairs.

Tate closed the door, pulled me back in, and again found my lips. Her kiss was urgent and demanding. I liked it.

She pulled back slightly. "I forgot the pizza."

"I've got cheese and crackers." I raised an eyebrow. "But it'll have to wait." I took her hand and led her to my bedroom.

It was dark when Tate's phone buzzed a few hours later. She rolled over and reached for it on the nightstand. I looked at the clock. It was seven p.m.

"Walker," Tate said in her detective voice, which was pretty cute since she was naked. She paused, then said, "Yeah, he's sending a message and escalating." A minute later, she said, "Thanks. I'll let her know."

She returned the phone to the nightstand, rolled back over, and laid an arm across my stomach. "That was Frank. They detonated the box."

I raised up on my elbow to look at her. A ray of moonlight shone from the window, highlighting her face. "And?"

She paused before going on. "It was full of playing cards and poker chips. No bomb."

I looked out the window. The full moon was bright orange. "It was Max bragging that he tied up my aunt and the others and set the fire."

"Yes," she said.

"Fuck!" I pounded the mattress with my fist and started to cry. "You have to catch him, Tate."

She pulled me to her and wrapped her warm body around mine. "I will, Riley. I promise."

I looked into her eyes, the moonlight highlighted how blue they were. "Before he kills someone."

She kissed me. I knew she wanted to promise me she would, but I also knew there was no way she could make that promise.

CHAPTER SEVENTEEN

Tate rarely slept in. Typically, she was gone by the time I got up. However, this morning, her hair disheveled, she walked out of the bedroom just before nine a.m., in her underwear and my Indigo Girls black T-shirt. It was tight on her, and it looked hot.

She yawned and stretched her arms over her head. "What time did you get up?" she asked as I set a cup of coffee in front of her.

"About an hour ago," I said, whisking batter for pancakes. "I thought I'd make pancakes for breakfast."

Tate paused her coffee mug halfway to her mouth and looked at me, her head cocked to the side.

"Don't look at me like that." I placed a skillet on the stove. "I know how to make pancakes." *I've watched Mom do it a thousand times. How hard can it be?*

She raised an eyebrow. "If you say so. What do you—" Her phone rang in the bedroom. "I'll be right back." She stood and walked into the bedroom, her ass teasing me as she walked away.

"This is Walker," she said, coming back into the kitchen. There were wrinkles on her forehead. I knew that look. Whatever it was, it wasn't good.

She didn't say anything for several minutes, just nodded and frowned. She looked at me, her lips pressed tightly together in a thin line.

She took a deep breath and let it out. "All right. I'll be there at noon." She ended the call and looked at me but paused before saying anything. I turned the heat off under the skillet. I wouldn't be making pancakes this morning.

"I have to go."

"I gathered that. What's going on?"

"Two guys on the narcotics team have Covid. They need me in the raid today."

My eyes widened. "The Lester Knight raid?"

"Yes. It's scheduled to go down at three o'clock, and there's a briefing at noon."

Her gaze dropped to the floor. "I'm sorry, Riley. I really wanted to spend the day with you."

I went to her and lifted her chin. Tears pooled in her eyes. "We'll spend tomorrow together. The more important thing is that you don't get hurt."

She wrapped her arms around my waist and pulled me to her, snuggling her face in the crook of my neck. "I'll be fine, don't worry. I'll be one of the last ones through the door."

I leaned my head on her shoulder and breathed in her scent. She smelled like sex. "When do you have to leave?"

"I have maybe an hour."

I stepped away and took her hand. "Then come back to bed with me."

Tate left an hour and a half later. We'd made love like it might be the last time we'd ever be together and then did it all over again in the shower.

I was going to need something to keep my mind off the raid and the possibility Tate could get hurt. I didn't want to think about all the ways things could go wrong, but my mind went there anyway. Someone could tip Knight off, the cops would be walking into an ambush, they could be outnumbered, there could be shooting, Tate could be shot. Tate could be... Nope, I wasn't going there. Tate would be fine.

I needed to do something. I needed to get out of my apartment and keep busy. I thought about going to my parents', but Aunt Liz was still in the hospital, so catching anyone at home would be hit or miss. We probably wouldn't be having a family dinner tonight either.

I called Patty. I hadn't talked to her since she went on leave. I sat down on the couch and called her number. After four rings, it went to voice mail, so I left a message.

I called Mike next. I wondered if he'd gone to the club the night before and performed after all the chaos here. After four rings, it went to voice mail. I didn't leave a message.

I thought about driving to Volumes of Pleasure in Los Osos. This small, independent, female-owned bookstore carried a good selection of sapphic literature. Then I remembered they were closed on Sundays. It was too bad because next door was a great bakery and one of the few places I knew of that made bierocks, an Eastern European pastry stuffed with ground beef, sauteed onions, and cabbage. Just thinking about it made my mouth water.

I settled for Barnes & Noble on Marsh Street. I could get a mocha and waste an hour or two checking out the recent lesfic offerings. I'd go there, then visit Aunt Liz in the hospital. Maybe by then I'd hear something from Tate.

In the hour and a half I'd been at B&N, I'd consumed an extra-large café mocha and a chocolate chip cookie. I stood in line at the register with the newest releases from Rita Potter, Lynnette Beers, newcomer KL Gallagher, and icon Karin Kallmaker when my phone vibrated. Patty's name popped up on the screen.

"Hi, Patty," I whispered, trying not to bother the people around me. I hate it when people talk loudly on their phones in public spaces. Nobody wants to hear your business. What don't they get?

"Hi, Riley." She sounded exhausted, and there were strange noises in the background.

"What's going on? You sound tired."

She chuckled. "Yeah, pushing out a baby will do that to you."

My eyes grew wide. "You had the baby? You're not due for three more weeks."

"We're both fine. Just tired."

"Did Dave make it back in time?" Dave, her husband, was a long-haul trucker who was on the road a lot.

"No, he missed another one. But he'll be here later today."

"Girl or a boy?" Patty and Dave had decided not to learn the sex of the baby ahead of time.

"A girl. Poor Tommy's going to be disappointed. He really wanted a little brother."

"What did you name her?"

"Adrian Riley."

I was speechless. *She named the baby after me?*

"You named her Riley?"

"Well, her middle name, anyway. Dave wanted Adrian, after his sister."

"I'm really honored, Patty. I didn't expect that." My eyes pooled with tears, and I wiped them away with one hand as I swiped my credit card at the register with the other.

"We've been through thick and thin, and you've always had my back. I can't think of a better name for her."

"Well, if I ever have a kid, I'll name it PJ. After you," I laughed. Patty's middle name was Jean.

"It? You're referring to your future child as *it*?"

"I doubt there's a kid in my future. But it's the thought that counts, right?"

"Right," she said.

"I'll let you get some rest. I'll come by in the morning, okay?"

"Sounds good. See you then."

I ended the call as I walked out of the store. My phone showed three o'clock. I took a deep breath and headed back to my car. I needed to stay busy, so I went to the hospital to visit my aunt.

When I arrived, the parking lot wasn't full. I guess Sunday afternoons aren't a busy time. Neither of my parents were there when I entered Aunt Liz's room, and she was sound asleep. I sat in the chair beside her bed and glanced at the television. *Diners, Drive-Ins, and Dives* was on, and Guy Fieri was pulling up to a food truck in his red Corvette. The volume had been turned down, so I couldn't hear where it was located.

I must have fallen asleep. The vibration of my phone in my pocket woke me, and I sat up. Aunt Liz was awake and smiling at me.

"Hello, sleepyhead," she said.

"Hi," I said, pulling my phone out of my pocket. It was Tate.

"I need to take this," I said, getting up. "I'll be right back." I walked out into the hallway.

"Tate, are you okay?" I could hear a lot of noise in the background but couldn't determine what it was.

"The raid didn't go exactly as planned, but we got Knight and most of his crew."

"Where are you? What's all that noise?"

"I don't want you to freak out. I was injured. It's not a big deal."

"Where are you?" My heart thumped so hard that I was surprised a nurse didn't stop to check on me.

"In the ER at your mom's hospital."

"I'll be right there." I hung up and hurried back to my aunt's room.

"Auntie, I have to run downstairs. Tate's been hurt. She says she's okay, but I need to go see for myself." I leaned down and kissed her on the cheek. "I'll be back later," I said, heading for the door.

CHAPTER EIGHTEEN

I raced to the elevator and pounded on the down button. The ten seconds it took for the doors to open seemed like ten hours. When I got to the first floor, I raced to the ER and asked where Tate was. Luckily, Mike's cabana boy, Timmy, walked by and told the woman behind the desk I was family, and he'd take me to her.

As we walked away, he grabbed my hand. "She's okay, Riley. She just needs a few stitches. You can start breathing again."

I gave him a small smile. *Stitches? What the hell happened?*

He led me to a cubicle with a dull green curtain around it and pulled it open. Tate sat back against the pillows, her feet up on the bed, holding a blood-soaked towel to her forehead. Her white T-shirt was covered in blood. When she saw me, one side of her mouth raised in a half-smile.

"How did you get here so fast?" she asked.

I walked in and sat on the edge of the bed. "I was upstairs visiting Aunt Liz. What the hell happened, Tate?"

"It probably looks a lot worse than it is. Head wounds bleed a lot."

"What happened?" I was getting frustrated with her evasiveness.

She took a deep breath. "A bullet grazed my forehead."

A bullet grazed her head? A fucking bullet grazed her head!

"How, Tate? How did that happen?" I know I sounded angry, but I was panicky. *What if the bullet...*

She grabbed my hand with her free hand. It had blood on it too.

"Take a breath. I know what's going through your head. Stop it. Stop thinking, 'What if.'"

"But—" Before I could argue, the same doctor who'd seen us yesterday walked in. I stood and went to the chair nearby.

"Tate, didn't I say I didn't want to see you back in my ER?" Dr. Ross said, pulling on blue rubber gloves.

"Hi, Dominique. You remember Riley, don't you?"

"Yes. Hello, Riley." She barely looked at me. "Okay, let's have a look." She took a large piece of gauze from a tray and held it near Tate's head as Tate removed the towel. The wound was two inches long and two inches above her left eye. The doctor pressed the gauze against it as blood began to ooze out.

"Hold this in place and keep pressure on it. You're lucky. Two inches lower and—"

"Yes, I know. I'm lucky I didn't lose an eye," Tate said, not looking at me.

Dr. Ross pursed her lips and nodded. "I can close it with sutures or glue. But even as good as I am, you'll have a scar." She paused briefly. "Glue's going to leave it a little jagged. Sutured would be cleaner. But it's up to you. Glue is painless. Sutures will hurt like hell, and you'll have to have a doctor take them out."

Tate looked at me.

I shrugged. "Are you worried about a scar?"

Tate shook her head. "Either way, I'm going to have one." Tate looked up at the doctor. "Let's go with glue. I've had enough pain for one day. I don't need any more."

"Unfortunately, you'll have a headache for a few days. We'll clean out the wound and give you a shot of antibiotics to prevent an infection. Other than the scar, there shouldn't be any lasting effects."

Tate nodded.

"I'll be back after the nurse cleans it out, then we'll close it up." She placed a hand on Tate's shoulder. I gritted my teeth and glared at her back.

"I'm glad it wasn't anything worse," she said.

"Yeah, me too." Tate leaned her head back on the bed.

"I'm going to inject some Novocain around the wound, so cleaning and closing won't be too painful." She picked up a hypodermic needle from the tray and began injecting small amounts in several places around the wound. "When's the last time you had a tetanus vaccine?" she asked when she was done.

"Last year. I stepped on glass at the beach."

I remembered that day. We'd gone to Avila Beach, and before we'd even spread a blanket out, a barefoot Tate stepped on a piece of clear glass hidden in the sand. I'd wrapped her foot in a beach towel and helped her hop back to the car.

"Good." Dr. Ross pulled off the blue latex gloves. "Okay, I'll be back in a little while to finish up." She dipped her head as she walked by me and left the cubicle.

I moved back to the bed and sat on the edge. "I really don't like her."

Tate chuckled. "Riley, we're just friends. We went out a few times a long time ago."

"How long ago?" I didn't know where this was coming from. Why was I jealous? I was the one putting roadblocks up, not wanting to formalize our relationship.

"I was a rookie cop, and she was doing her residency here." She looked up at the ceiling and then back at me. "That was five years ago."

That didn't make me feel any better. I've read plenty of second-chance romances. I decided right then that I didn't like that genre.

She took my hands in hers. "There's no need to be jealous."

"What? I'm not jealous." *Maybe I was, just a little.*

"Okay, if you say so."

Before I could respond, my mother, wearing pink scrubs, entered, holding a tray. "Ready for me to clean it out?"

I stood and stepped away from the bed to make room for her.

"Hi, Mrs. Reynolds," Tate said.

"Tate, you're practically family. It's okay to call me Angela." She set the tray on the little table next to the bed.

"Okay, Angela." Tate smiled and winked at me.

"Mom, I didn't expect to see you here."

"I work here, remember." She leaned over Tate and removed the gauze from her forehead. The blood had slowed.

"Yes, but not on Sundays."

"Several people are out with Covid, so I'm filling in."

"I don't want to be in the way. I'll go get a cup of coffee." I stood.

"What, you don't want to watch your mother torture me?" Tate asked with a grin.

I shrugged. "I'm thirsty. Can I bring you anything?"

"A Dr. Pepper if you can find one," Tate said.

"You got it. Mom, do you want anything?"

"No thanks, I just came off a break."

"Okay, I'll be back soon."

On my way out of the ER, I ran into Timmy pushing an elderly man in a wheelchair.

"How's she doing?" he asked.

"She'll be fine. The bullet grazed her forehead."

"She's lucky."

"Don't I know it."

"I gotta get this guy to x-ray. I'm glad she's okay." He gave me a quick hug and began pushing the wheelchair down the hall.

When I returned to the cubicle, my mother was gone, and there was a large bandage on Tate's forehead. Dr. Ross was sitting on the edge of the bed with her hand on Tate's leg. I walked around to the other side of the bed, handed Tate her soda, took her hand, and smiled at the doctor.

Tate smiled up at me. "I'm good to go."

Dr. Ross stood and put her hands in the pockets of her white lab coat. "Take it easy for at least a week, and no work. You should limit your alcohol intake for a few days, and you shouldn't be left alone for twenty-four hours." She turned to me. "I assume you can take care of that?"

"Of course."

She turned back to Tate. "The glue will dissolve on its own in two to three weeks." She turned to leave, then turned back. "I'm glad you're okay," she said to Tate, then looked at me. "Take care of her."

I nodded. "I will."

"A nurse will be here shortly to wheel you out," she said, then left.

It was past six when we got back to my apartment. We were both exhausted.

"Are you hungry?" I asked.

"No. I think the adrenaline's worn off. I'm exhausted." She dropped onto a kitchen chair.

"Why don't you go clean up?" The blood on her shirt and pants had dried and turned rust-colored.

"Yeah, good idea." She stood and slowly shuffled down the hall.

Twenty minutes later, she emerged in a pair of gray sweats and a SLO Brew T-shirt. She held her bloody clothes in a bundle. "I think we can throw these away. They'll never come clean."

I retrieved a plastic shopping bag from under the sink and held it open. "Put them in here, and I'll take them to the trash can later."

She dropped them into the bag and I set it outside. When I came back, she was leaning against the wall. "I'm going to go lay down if that's okay."

"Of course, it's okay."

We'd been lying in bed for almost an hour, talking about anything other than death, when Tate rolled onto her side to face me. She looked into my eyes but didn't say anything.

I reached out and ran a finger over her lips. "These are perfect for kissing."

She leaned in and gently kissed me. "You mean like that?"

My lips were less than an inch from hers. "Just like that," I whispered. I placed my hand behind her neck and pulled her to me. My kiss was urgent this time. Her lips parted, and my tongue entered, the kiss became heated. My heart raced as the kiss deepened and our tongues explored one another. I paused and pulled back just far enough to look at her. "The doctor said you should take it easy."

"I can't think of anything easier than this." She reached for the top button on my shirt. "This needs to go," she said, undoing the button, then another and another.

My breathing quickened as I watched her long, slender fingers make their way down my shirt. When the last button was undone, I sat up and removed it, revealing my black bra. Tate reached around my back, unhooked it, pulled the straps off my shoulders, and tossed it on the floor. Then she sat up, pulled her shirt over her head, and dropped it on the floor. She wasn't wearing a bra.

I took a deep breath, admiring her perfect breasts. With the tip of her finger, she traced a path from the base of my neck to my belly button. "You're beautiful," she whispered.

I smiled, feeling vulnerable yet excited by how she looked at me. Without saying a word she kissed me, our hands moving hungrily over each other's curves. When Tate brushed her fingertips across one of my nipples, sparks went straight to the depths of my core.

I tugged at the waist of her sweatpants. "It's time for these to go."

"Your wish is my command." She pulled them off as I wiggled out of mine. She lay back beside me, taking a nipple into her mouth again, and expertly sucked it. A moan escaped from somewhere, and I realized it was me. She released my nipple and slowly kissed her way down to the V between my legs. She licked my erect nub, teasing me. My body trembled. I grabbed hold of her hair, careful not to touch the bandage on her forehead.

"Tate, please, inside."

She complied, pushing two fingers inside. "You're so wet," she said as she moved in and out in a gentle rhythm.

"More," I begged. She inserted a third finger and thrust deeper. Waves of pleasure enveloped me. The intensity was almost more than I could bear. Perhaps our brushes with death had profoundly affected both of us. I put that out of my mind as wave after wave kept coming until it peaked, and I fell back against the bed, panting.

As my orgasm faded, I held tightly to Tate, afraid to let her go. As we lay together, breathing heavily, I tried not to think about how close I'd come to losing her. For the first time, I realized I couldn't imagine my life without her in it.

When I'd regained my senses, I opened my eyes. Tate looked down at me, smiling.

"That was amazing," I said, still feeling the aftereffects.

"You're amazing." Her voice was husky with emotion.

I squeezed my eyes shut, ordering my tears to stay put. When I opened them, she was still looking at me. Tears threatened to spill from her eyes. I pushed everything else aside—the fire, Tate's brush with death, and the madman who wanted to kill me. At least for now, locked in this room, wrapped in each other's arms, we were safe.

CHAPTER NINETEEN

When I woke up Monday morning, Tate was already out of bed. I rolled over and looked at the clock on the nightstand. Seven thirty. I grabbed a sweatshirt off the back of the bedroom door and put it on before I went to look for her. I found her sorting laundry in the bathroom.

I stood in the doorway and crossed my arms. "What do you think you're doing?"

She jumped a half foot in the air. "Jesus, you scared the shit out of me."

"Good." I raised an eyebrow and stared at her. "Whatever you're doing isn't taking it easy."

She rolled her eyes. "I don't think doing laundry will tax my head too much."

I took hold of her hand and pulled her out of the bathroom and down the hall to the kitchen. "Come on, I'll make you breakfast."

"Hah," she laughed. "You're out of cereal."

"I'll make toast after I call work. I'm staying home today."

"I don't need babysitting."

"Yes, you do," I said over my shoulder as I went to find my phone. Tate wasn't good at resting or taking it easy. Left alone she might mow the lawn, plant a tree and paint the living room. It wasn't in her nature to lie around and do nothing, even if injured.

Luckily Stan was out of the office. I left a message with the receptionist that I had a migraine and was staying home. After the weekend I'd had, no one would be surprised if I did.

When I returned to the kitchen, Tate sat at the table talking to someone on her phone. I started the toast and retrieved butter and jam from the refrigerator. While I waited, I poured myself a cup of coffee and refilled Tate's mug.

The toast popped up a minute later, just as Tate ended the call. "That was Sue Skylar."

"What did she want so early in the morning?"

"She was looking for you, actually."

My head shot up and I spread jam all over my fingers. "What? Why did she call you?"

Tate laughed. "She called your office, and they said you weren't in." Tate raised a shoulder. "So she tried me."

I frowned. "What did she want?"

"During questioning last night, one of Knight's crew rolled over on him. The guy agreed to a plea bargain to stay out of prison. Among other things, she said Knight killed Archie Abercrombie in retaliation for chopping up his daughter's car."

I put the toast on a plate and set it on the counter in front of Tate.

"So, Pinky's no longer a suspect?"

She took a bite of toast. "She's off the hook for the murder, but if Knight knows she stole his daughter's car, she may want to sleep with one eye open."

"I should call her and let her know she can stop hiding." I bit into the other piece of toast.

Tate leaned in and licked blueberry jam off my lips. "It can wait." She smiled, took my hand, and led me down the hallway.

I should have gotten up the first time the alarm went off the next morning, for sure, the second time. But no, I waited until it screamed at me a third time. Now I was running thirty minutes late, and I still had to go by my place and change clothes.

Not only should I have gotten up on time, but I should have grabbed an umbrella from the closet by my front door before I rushed down the stairs. *How did I not know it was raining?* Water trickled down my back, and I swore out loud as I climbed into my car. Where the hell did the rain come from? It wasn't supposed to rain in California in September.

I closed the car door and turned the key, the only noise other than the sound of rain hitting the roof was the click, click, click of a dead battery.

"Damn it!" I pounded my hand on the dashboard. Stan was going to have a fit.

I grabbed my phone and started to call Tate, then remembered she wasn't supposed to be driving. Mike's car wasn't in the driveway, so he'd already left for work. I brought up my parents' number and pushed the green button. After two rings, Aunt Liz picked up. Shit, I'd forgotten to go back and see her in the hospital Sunday night.

"Aunt Liz, when did you get home?"

"Around nine Sunday night." She yawned. "It was nice to sleep in my bed and in a gown that doesn't show off my fanny."

"I'll bet. How do you feel?"

"I'm still coughing and don't remember much." I heard her take a slurp of her coffee. "How's Tate?"

"She's lucky. The bullet grazed her forehead. Two inches lower, and she could have lost an eye."

"I'll bet she's got one hell of a headache."

"Yeah, it was pretty bad yesterday," I said. "Hey, Aunt Liz, is my dad around? My battery's dead, and I need a ride."

"Sorry, kiddo, your mom and dad both left. But if you can give me time to change my clothes, I'll take you."

"I don't think you should be out running around yet, do you?"

"The doctor said to take it easy. I can drive a few miles without exerting too much."

"Okay. Thanks, Auntie."

"Give me fifteen minutes."

I thanked her again and ended the call, relieved that I wouldn't have to call Tate. I decided to wait in the car and listen to *The Lesbian Review* podcast rather than go back inside. No sense getting drenched twice. As I sat there, the rain steadily pounding on the roof, I started to feel like I was being watched. What if Max Maynard was lurking nearby, just waiting for me to step out of the car? I shook it off, I wasn't going to let him get in my head any more than he already was.

Fifteen minutes later, Aunt Liz pulled up in her silver 2010 Ford Focus, a bright-purple scarf wrapped around her neck. She smiled as I climbed into the passenger seat.

"Thanks, Aunt Liz, I owe you one."

"Riley, you saved my life. Let's call it even." She put the car in drive, then looked at me and winked.

Traffic was light through downtown. We hit all the green lights, and I was only an hour late when we pulled up in front of my office. I thanked her for coming to my rescue and climbed out of the silver bullet.

"Anytime." She smiled and drove off, leaving a cloud of exhaust in her wake.

I entered the building, hoping I wouldn't run into Stan before I'd had a chance to grab a cup of coffee. I wasn't that lucky. He was in the lobby, waiting for me with an accusatory look on his face.

"You're late."

I decided to go with honesty. "My car battery was dead, and I had to call my aunt to give me a ride. I'm really sorry."

"Not surprising considering the piece of crap you drive," he said. "Where are you with the stack of warrants I gave you?"

I sighed. As much as I didn't want to admit it, he was right. My car was a piece of shit. But it was my piece of shit, and it was paid for.

"Two of them are dead. One OD'd a year ago, and the other was hit by a train."

"How did that happen?"

"Apparently, he had headphones on and didn't hear it." I shrugged. "I found out one of them, Eddie Easter, is dealing out of his house. I alerted Atascadero PD. They'll use our warrant to enter and search the place. Who knows what they'll find?"

He turned and headed back to his office. "Okay, that's three. What about the other seven?"

"One of the women is in custody in Nevada. She went there to get married and was pulled over for drunk driving on the strip. When the cops ran her name, the warrant came up. They're holding her until our sheriff's office can go get her." I paused and took a deep breath. "I'm still working on the other six."

He dropped into his chair and opened a white McDonald's bag. "Okay, keep me updated. I want the others found this week." He pulled an Egg McMuffin out of the bag like it was a rabbit out of a hat and looked up at me. "That's it." He took a humongous bite and chewed with his mouth open. "And don't forget you have an hour to make up."

I retreated to my office, the smell of Egg McMuffin making my mouth water. My chair squealed when I sat down, and I reminded myself to bring a can of WD40 to work. It wasn't worth putting in a work order. I'd just do it myself. I drummed my fingers on the desk. I knew I needed to get to work but I was having a hard time focusing. My foot bounced up and down as I stared at the wall and thought about Max Maynard. What would he do next? There was no way to know. I was going to have to trust Tate and her department to stop him before he got to me.

I took in the giant stack of files on my desk, stretched my neck from side to side and opened the first one. Anthony Anderson had been arrested three times. The first time for possessing and selling counterfeit concert tickets. The second time he broke into a sporting goods store and stole a dozen rifles. Most recently, he'd been pulled over by a sheriff's deputy for not wearing a seatbelt. When the deputy ran his ID, it came up that he was on probation, so the deputy searched his car and found a ghost gun in the trunk. It's illegal for a convicted felon to have a firearm. Anderson did a year in county jail for the gun and violating his probation. He'd been released from jail over a year ago. He never reported to the probation department, and a warrant was issued six months ago.

I made a note of his last known address. Ironically, it was in the same rundown trailer park in Atascadero as Eddie Easter. I wrote another note to check with the Atascadero PD to see if they'd raided Easter's trailer yet.

I continued to review files until I couldn't ignore the growling in my stomach any longer. I slid my arms into my still-wet jacket and headed for the door. Outside the rain had turned into a drizzle. I pulled my hood over my head and jogged to my probation car parked at the far end of the lot and headed for Burrito-Burrito. After the morning I'd had, I deserved it.

I'd just finished paying when my phone buzzed. It was Tate. "Hi. Is everything okay?"

"Yeah. I'm fine. My headache's better, thank God." She paused. "What are you wearing?" she whispered.

WTF? Did Tate really just ask me what I was wearing?

I walked away from the counter and stood near the door to wait for my order. "I am not engaging in phone sex with you right now. I'm working."

"You're no fun," she laughed. "What are you doing?"

"Picking up a burrito and coffee. Then I need to follow up on a couple of warrants. What are your plans?"

"Since I can't drive, my options are limited. I guess I could vacuum, and clean out the refrigerator."

"Burrito for Riley," the guy behind the counter yelled.

I grabbed the bag and coffee and stepped out onto the sidewalk. The rain had stopped, and the sun was trying to push through the clouds.

"Do you want me to bring you lunch later?" I asked as I walked to my car.

"That'd be great. I'll take the Listen Linda with the works from Mr. Pickle."

"All right. I'll see ya around one."

I ended the call and climbed into the car. I unwrapped one end of the burrito and the aroma of eggs and potatoes fried in butter greeted me. The first bite was almost orgasmic. My taste buds were in heaven. Then the phone buzzed. It was an unknown number, so I let it go to voice mail. If it was important, whoever it was would leave a message. As I sat there chewing, I scanned my surroundings. It was only ten thirty, so the lunch crowd hadn't invaded downtown yet. In an hour the streets and sidewalks would be packed with hungry people looking for a quick meal. I tried to avoid this part of town at lunchtime and on weekends. Parking was impossible and the crowds were a pain in the ass.

After two bites of the burrito, I set it on the passenger seat and started the car. Holding the coffee in one hand, I pulled out onto the one-way street. I took a left on Broad and headed back to the office. I took a sip of coffee as I waited at the stoplight at Broad and Pacific. I glanced over to the patio in front of Libertine Brewing Company. It didn't open for another fifteen minutes, so they weren't seating anyone yet, but a guy with a shaved head was smoking a cigarette at one of the tables. I'll be damned if it wasn't Max Maynard. I didn't notice the light turn green, the person behind me laid on his horn, which got Max's attention. The second he spotted my probation car, he flung the cigarette aside, hopped the waist-high wrought iron fence that surrounded the patio, and took off down Pacific like a conspiracy theory being chased by the truth. For a big guy, he was fast and agile.

I slid my coffee into the cup holder and took off after him. When he rounded the corner at Garden, I was half a block behind him, my rear tires squealing as I took the turn, and my burrito flew off the seat onto the floor. Damn it, he'd pay for that.

I followed him down an alley between two small houses, but I had to slow to avoid the dumpsters. The last I saw of him, he'd vaulted over a fence and was gone, like a rat down a hole.

I exited the alley and pulled to the curb, my heart racing. It took several minutes for my breathing to return to normal. I looked down at the burrito. The contents were splattered across the floorboard. I sighed, sipped my now-cold coffee, and called police dispatch to give them a heads-up. Maybe they'd have better luck than I'd had.

I was too keyed up to go back to the office and sit behind a desk, so I drove to Mr. Pickles and ordered Tate's sandwich. While I waited, I checked the voice mail from earlier. It was Bud letting me know he'd be back at work on Wednesday. He'd been cleared to leave the office but he couldn't qualify with a firearm until the cast came off.

It was good news. I smiled. If Patty and I were Cagney and Lacey, Bud and I would be Batwoman and Robin. I texted him back:

Get ready for the queer dynamic duo!

A minute later, he replied:

I'm Robin!

I texted back:

Obviously.

"Order for Riley," the young woman with a pierced tongue called out.

I thanked her, took the bag, and walked to my car. It was almost noon, so traffic had picked up, and I hit every red light. The bacon on the Listen Linda Sando made my mouth water, and I cursed at the loss of another breakfast burrito.

I pulled to the curb in front of Tate's olive-green-and-black ranch-style house. I grabbed the bag and headed to the door. Before I could knock, the door opened, and Tate stood there looking like she'd just rolled out of bed. Her messy hair was a turn-on, the baggy sweatpants not so much, but she was braless under the threadbare tank top, so I wasn't complaining.

I handed over the bag. "You look hot, babe."

She smiled half-heartedly, took the bag, and stepped aside to let me in. "If you think this is sexy, you should see me without the bandage on my forehead." She closed the door and headed to the kitchen table. "The scar isn't going to be pretty."

I winked. "It'll be hot on you."

She opened the bag, pulled out the sandwich, and took a huge bite. "Thanks for this. I'm not really up to going shopping," she said with her mouth full.

"No problem." I took a seat across from her. "How about I pick up a few things for you on my way home? I could even make dinner."

The sandwich was halfway to her mouth, but she stopped and looked at me but didn't say anything.

I shrugged. "I make excellent mac and cheese."

She let out a laugh. "What about a protein and vegetable?"

I crossed my arms. "Cheese is a protein." I stuck out my tongue. "And if you insist on a vegetable, I'll get a bag of lettuce and ranch dressing."

She shook her head. "You're ridiculous. But sure." She took another bite of the sandwich before asking, "Anything interesting going on?"

I leaned the chair back on two legs. "Well, I had a run-in with Max this morning."

She put the sandwich down and stared at me. "You what?"

"Well, not a run-in, more like a chase."

Her eyebrows shot up. "He chased you?"

"No, I chased him. In my car."

"What?"

"After I talked to you, I headed back to work. I was stopped at Broad and Pacific and looked over at the patio in front of Libertine. He was sitting there smoking a cigarette." I shook my head. "When the guy behind me honked, Max looked up, saw me, and took off running. So, I took off after him. I lost him when he jumped over a fence at Garden Street. I also lost my burrito."

She pursed her lips. "You should have called the police."

"I don't think they'd care about the burrito," I said with a straight face, then smiled. "It happened so fast I didn't have time to think. I just reacted. But I did call them after."

She sighed and shook her head. "I'll call the lieutenant and request additional patrols downtown." She got up and took the empty paper bag to the trash can. "I think you should stay here tonight."

"Sure. But I have to get the battery on my car charged first. It's dead."

"Dead?"

"Yeah. When I got in it to go to work, it was dead as a doornail." I shrugged.

"Did you check the cables?"

I shook my head. "It was pouring rain, and I was already late. Aunt Liz gave me a ride."

I pulled my keys out of my pocket. "After I stop at the grocery, I'll go by my place, feed Randolph, and grab some clothes for tomorrow."

She walked back and wrapped her arms around me. "Be careful, okay?"

"I will, don't worry."

"As long as he's out there, I'll worry."

After a quick kiss, I was out the door and on my way back to work.

The rest of the day dragged by painfully slow. I kept thinking about the look on Max's face when he saw me. He was surprised but not afraid.

Stan left at four, so I didn't stay the extra hour. As soon as he pulled out of the parking lot, I called an Uber for a ride to the grocery store near the office. I picked up the ingredients for mac and cheese, lettuce and ranch dressing. I also picked up a few things to keep Tate fed until she got the all-clear to drive. Then I called another Uber to take me home.

When I got to my place, I walked up the stairs hugging a bag of groceries with each arm. I set one down and reached into my pocket to get my key. A loud thump at the bottom of the stairs drew my attention. A figure, all in black, stood there. It was Max.

"You thought you had me today, didn't ya, bitch?" He took a step up the stairs. My firearm was locked in the trunk of my car. I'd forgotten to get it out when Aunt Liz picked me up. All I had was a canister of pepper spray. I set the other bag down and reached for the little red can clipped to my belt and held it behind my back. My heart began to race, and I breathed deeply to keep my panic at bay. I needed to wait until he got close enough to hit him full in the face. Luckily there wasn't any wind to blow it back at me.

He grasped the railing and took another step up the stairs. The scar on his forearm from the long-ago fire glowed an angry red. "You always thought you were so smart." There was no humor in his laugh. "Who's the smart one, now?"

He took another step up the stairs.

"What do you want, Max?" I tried to keep my voice steady. He wanted to make me afraid. He was doing a good job of it.

"Couldn't start your car this morning, could ya?" He took another step up. "I disconnected the battery." He was on the fourth step, eight to the top.

Blood pounded in my ears. I breathed in and out slowly to calm myself. I couldn't give in to the fear.

He took another step: seven to go. I forced myself to wait until he took two, preferably three more steps. I'd only get one chance.

"I was gunna grab you, tie you up and set fire to your house. With you in it."

Thank God it had been raining, or I might have gotten out to check under the hood.

He climbed two more steps. I pulled the canister from behind my back and aimed it at his face. Just as I pressed down on the top of the canister, Mike's porch light lit up the driveway, and Mike walked out his back door. He held the red baseball bat like he was ready to hit a home run. Max twisted his body away from me to glare at Mike just as the green gel, rated 1,250,000 on the Scoville heat scale, shot over his shoulder, barely missing him.

"Riley, what's going on?" Mike yelled.

I never took my eyes off Max. He glared at me and snarled, "Next time, bitch." Then he jumped to the bottom of the stairs and took off like the hounds of hell were chasing him.

My knees gave out. I fell against the door and slid to the ground. Two run-ins with Max Maynard on the same day was two too many.

Mike flew up the stairs and knelt beside me, the bat still in his hand. "Riley, are you okay? Who was that?"

"The maniac who wants to kill me." I tried to stand, but my legs didn't want to cooperate. "Can you help me up?"

He put his free hand around my upper arm and pulled me up. My hand shook as I clipped the pepper spray back on my belt and unlocked the door. We hurried into the apartment, and I locked it behind us.

"Mike, would you call the police and tell them what happened?" I set the groceries on the counter and collapsed into a kitchen chair. I focused on Randolph swimming around in his watery world, ignorant of what had happened on the other side of the door.

Once my heartbeat returned to normal, I fed Randolph, then called Tate. She insisted on a play-by-play of what happened. Of course, she wanted to jump on her motorcycle and race over. I reminded her she wasn't cleared to drive, especially a motorcycle. I assured her Mike would stay with me until the police arrived. While we waited, I took two beers from the fridge and handed one to Mike. My hands shook, and Mike had to unscrew the top for me.

Surprisingly, it only took the police twenty minutes to arrive. After we gave them our statements and they left, we walked down to my car. I raised the hood to reattach the cables, but I was still shaky, and Mike did it for me. The car started right up. I thanked Mike, gave him a hug then went to the trunk and retrieved my gun.

By the time I got to Tate's it was after eight. I was exhausted and in no condition to cook. Tate, guessing what shape I'd be in, had thought ahead and a pizza was on the table when I arrived. I didn't even question myself when I thought about what I great girlfriend she was.

CHAPTER TWENTY

Rain poured down again Wednesday morning. Tate handed me an umbrella as I left the house, so I wasn't too drenched when I got to my car. Luckily it started up without an issue. When I walked into my office, Bud was sitting at his desk, buried behind a wall of files, all I could see of him was from the eyes up.

He looked over the mountain of files. "Girl, you look like a drowned rat."

"It's raining again. It's September. It's not supposed to be raining." I leaned the umbrella behind the door to dry, peeled off my jacket, and hung it on the coat rack by the door, then grabbed a napkin from my desk drawer and wiped my face.

"It's been in the forecast all week." He leaned back in his chair.

"I've had a shitty few days. Checking the weather report wasn't a priority." I took a brush from the desk and tried to make my hair look presentable.

"What happened?"

I gave up on my hair and tossed the brush back in the drawer. "Let's see. Early Saturday morning Max Maynard set fire to McGee's Pub and almost killed my aunt. Tate and I found her, Judge Bookings, and two others and dragged them out."

"What the fuck? Are they okay?"

"My aunt's fine. They kept her overnight and let her go home Monday morning. I haven't heard anything about the judge or the other two."

"Shit!" he swore. "I was out of town until yesterday. I didn't hear anything about it."

"Oh wait, it gets better." I held up my hand. "On Sunday, Tate got called in to help on a raid and got shot."

"Shot? Oh my God. Is she all right?"

"Yeah. She was lucky that it just grazed her forehead." I paused and rubbed my eyes. "A little lower, and she could have lost an eye. Or worse." I took a deep breath. "Then yesterday I came across Max and chased him all over downtown."

His eyes almost bugged out. "Did you catch him?"

"No. He jumped over a fence and that was the last I saw of him." I dropped into my chair. "Then Max was waiting for me when I got home last night."

"What?" He almost jumped out of his chair. "What happened?"

I gave him the details, starting with the dead battery and ending with Mike scaring Max off. Reliving it only made the nightmare more real. I needed to think about something else. I picked up the Anderson file from yesterday. "I need to get out of here. I'm going to go look for this guy."

"Can I go with you?" He flashed me a mischievous grin. "Stan's in a meeting at the courthouse. He won't be back until after lunch."

"I guess what he doesn't know won't hurt us." I grabbed my wet jacket from the coat rack. "Come on, Boy Wonder, let's look for a bad guy."

"Good thing I wore my yellow crime-fighting tights under my pants today."

"You're what?"

He pulled on his probation jacket. "You know...Robin always wore yellow tights and a red vest when he and Batman fought crime."

I shook my head. "Just keep your pants on, okay?"

The rain had stopped by the time we drove into the mobile home park. At the far end, red lights flashed on three Atascadero PD vehicles parked in front of Eddie Easter's space. A half dozen cops wandered in and out of the trailer. The old woman I'd spoken to the other day sat in her rocking chair on her front porch, watching the goings-on down the street. I pulled into the parking space across the street, cut the engine, and turned to Bud.

"That's Eddie Easter's trailer. I was here last week looking for him. That woman on the porch said he was dealing out of the trailer, so I let the PD know. Looks like they chose today to raid the place. I'm going to talk to her. Stay here and keep an eye out for Anderson. There's a picture of him in the file."

"But I'm your wingman," he protested.

"Yeah, and my wingman needs to watch for Anderson."

He glared at me but didn't argue. I climbed out of the car and crossed the street.

"Good morning." I stood on the first step up to her porch. "Lots of excitement today."

She nodded. "Yep. They pulled in an hour ago, broke open the front door, and rushed in."

I leaned against the handrail. "Was he in there?"

She cackled, "Nope. He's hiding over there behind that dumpster." She pointed to the beat-up green-and-rust industrial dumpster halfway between her space and Eddie Easter's trailer.

I looked to where she pointed. "You're kidding me."

"No, I ain't. He ran out of that trailer a minute before the cops showed up, wearing nothing but a pair of boxers." She slapped her thigh and laughed out loud. "He ducked behind the dumpster just as the cops turned the corner down the street."

"Well, I'll be damned." I stepped into the street to get a better look at the dumpster. "I guess I could sneak up behind him and arrest him."

She continued to rock back and forth. "Yep, I guess you could."

I walked back to my car and opened the door. "She says Easter's hiding behind that dumpster. I'm going to sneak up behind him."

"Let me help."

I shook my head. "No way."

"Pleeease." He clasped his hands together, looking like a kid begging to ride the biggest roller coaster at the fair.

"You have handcuffs?"

Bud nodded enthusiastically. "In my pocket."

"Okay, let's go." He climbed out of the car, and we surreptitiously walked toward the dumpster forty feet away. When we got closer, I stopped Bud and whispered, "I want you to walk to the front of the dumpster and surprise him. I'll be at the back waiting for him to run."

Bud nodded, and we continued toward the dumpster without a word. When we were five yards away, I motioned for Bud to go to the front of the dumpster, and I waited behind it with pepper spray in one hand.

"Mr. Easter, I'm—" Before Bud could finish, Easter shoved him. Bud fell backward and landed on his ass. Easter shot around the end of the dumpster. He paused when he saw me standing there with pepper spray pointed at him. His eyes darted every which way, looking for a way around me.

"You're under—" He slammed into me, laying me out on the ground, the pepper spray flying out of my hand. "Fuck! Bud, he's running!"

I rolled over and took off after Easter. Bud had already gotten to his feet and was a few steps ahead of me. Easter sprinted down the street, his pink boxers waving in the breeze. As we neared the old lady's porch, a stick flew out of nowhere, tripping Easter. He flew forward, crashed to the ground, and rolled over twice. Bud got to him first. Easter, his hands, elbows, and knees bleeding, tried to sit up and push Bud away. I ran up and forced Easter to the ground with my foot on his back. Bud sat on Easter and looked up at me with a huge grin.

"Can I handcuff him?"

"He's all yours, Robin."

Bud took handcuffs from his pocket and slapped one bracelet on Easter's right wrist and the other on his left. He'd been practicing.

I walked over to the stick that tripped up Easter. It was a walking cane. I picked it up and strolled over to the old woman's porch, twirling the cane like a baton. "Did you lose this?"

She grinned. "Yes, I did. Thanks for returning it." She held out an age-spotted hand.

I handed it over. "My pleasure."

I returned to Bud and helped him lift Easter off the ground. "Let's drive him down the street and hand him over to the cops. If they book him on drug charges, the jail will hold him longer than on our warrant." I opened the car's back door, and Bud helped Easter in. "If you're nice to them, maybe they'll let you put pants on before they take you in," I said to Easter.

He grumbled, something about my parentage, I think. I gave him a big smile before I closed the door.

It was a short drive to the other end of the street. I pulled up behind one of the cop cars. "I'll go talk to them. You wait here with Mr. Easter."

I got out of the car, walked to the closest officer, and identified myself. He directed me to Sergeant Jackson, the officer in charge of the raid. Making sure my badge was clearly visible, I entered the trailer. The sergeant stood in the middle of the living room. Two other officers were in the tiny kitchen pulling out drawers and opening cabinets. The place looked like a tornado had blown through, and there were two handguns, a box of ammunition, a scale, and at least a dozen small packets of a white powdery substance lying on the coffee table. A disheveled, middle-aged man with swollen red eyes and thick stubble on his face sat on the floor, his hands handcuffed behind his back. He looked familiar but I couldn't place him.

"Who the hell are you?" the sergeant barked.

I held out my hand. "Riley Reynolds, I'm with the probation department." He looked at my hand but didn't take it, so I shoved it into my jacket pocket.

He glared at me. "Why are you standing in my crime scene?"

"I'm the one who notified your department about the warrant and the drugs."

"So?"

Jeez, what an asshole. "I was in the area looking for another probationer and came across Eddie Easter hiding down the street. I thought you might want him."

The sergeant's eyes bugged out of his head. "You. Have. Easter?" He spit out each word.

I smiled. "Yes. He's handcuffed and sitting in the back of my car." I crossed my arms. "I thought you'd want to book him. If I book him on the probation warrant, the jail will probably give him a citation to appear in court and let him go."

He stared at me. I could tell he was grinding his teeth. "Fine. I'll trade you."

My eyebrows grew together. "Trade for what?"

He motioned to the guy on the ground. "Him. He has a probation warrant."

I looked at the guy on the floor. His lip curled on one side in a snarl. "Who's he?"

"Anthony Anderson."

I swallowed a laugh. What a coincidence. "You don't want him for the drugs?"

"No. The idiot was standing on the porch when we pulled up. He wasn't inside the trailer, so we can't connect him. We searched him. He doesn't have anything on him. He claims he was looking for his cat."

I didn't see the need to tell the sergeant that Anderson was who I'd come out here to look for. I'd be happy to let him think I was doing him a favor. I smiled. "Sure, I'll take him off your hands." It only took a few minutes to get Easter out of my car, switch handcuffs on the two, put Anderson in the back of my car, and Easter in one of the cop cars. As the door of the cop car closed, I heard Easter yell something about his pants. I smiled to myself and drove away.

The jail wasn't busy when we arrived, and we were able to book Anderson and get out of there in less than thirty minutes. An all-time record.

We got back to the office at 1:15, a full ten minutes before Stan, who stopped at our office before heading to his own. He held a McDonald's sack in one hand and a thirty-two-ounce cup in the other. I wondered if the soda was diet.

He ignored Bud and looked at me. "Did you serve those warrants?"

I leaned back in my chair and casually flipped a pen around my fingers. I smiled sweetly. "As a matter of fact, Stan, two of them were booked this morning."

He frowned. "You caught two of them this morning?"

"Well, to be honest, I caught one and assisted Atascadero PD with the other." I winked at Bud.

"Good." He walked away without saying another word.

I shook my head and threw the pen down. "Just once, it'd be nice to hear 'Good job, Riley,' or 'Nice work, Riley.'"

Bud laughed. "There's always tomorrow."

I stared daggers at him. "Shut up, Robin."

CHAPTER TWENTY-ONE

I'd left Randolph home alone for two nights and was feeling guilty, so we spent the night at my place. I also needed to do laundry, or I'd be going commando tomorrow. Tate still couldn't drive so I picked her up on my way home. Fortunately, knowing my refrigerator was probably empty, she brought the ingredients I'd left at her house to make mac and cheese.

After I tossed a load of whites in the washer, I threw dinner together, including a required vegetable: bagged lettuce and bottled ranch dressing. Tate, in baggy sweatpants, loose-fitting tank top, bare feet, and a clean bandage on her forehead, walked into the kitchen and looked out the window, then checked to make sure it was locked. Then she did the same in the living room before returning to the kitchen. The bruising from the wound on her forehead had seeped down around her eye, but she was still sexy as hell. I tried to ignore the heat radiating from her and concentrate on the salad, but the pull was too strong to resist. I took a few steps closer and wrapped my arms around her waist. We stayed like that, our bodies pressed together, my head resting on her chest, until the timer dinged a few minutes later. She slowly pulled away.

"I'm starving," she said then kissed the top of my head before letting go.

"It's ready. Have a seat and I'll dish it up."

I plated our dinner then took a seat across from her. We ate in silence for a few minutes before she stopped and looked at me. "You really do make the best mac and cheese I've ever had." She grinned and took another bite.

I winked at her. "It's all in the cheese."

She laughed and we finished our dinner in a comfortable silence. When we were done, she cleared the table while I cleaned up the kitchen. As I dried the last pot I felt her arms wrap around my waist from behind.

"Thank you for dinner." She kissed my neck.

I turned and smiled at her. "Anytime." We stood there looking into each other's eyes before she leaned forward and kissed me softly. I felt a warmth spread through my body as our lips met, and her tongue sought mine. I closed my eyes to savor the moment, and an unexpected tear rolled down my cheek. It hit me just how close I'd come to losing her.

I stepped out of her embrace and brushed away the tear. "Come on, let's watch a movie."

She smiled and nodded then took my hand in hers and led me into the living room. We sat on the couch, and I put on a movie. I smiled to myself as she snuggled closer and laid her head on my shoulder. At least for now, with her here next to me, I felt safe.

Something woke me from an exhausted sleep. I looked at the clock on the nightstand, 2:15. The moon was gone, and the room was pitch black. Tate, naked, spooned me from behind. I smiled at the cute little noises she made in her sleep. Then I heard a rustling sound. I couldn't tell where it was coming from. I didn't want to, but I extricated myself from Tate's embrace and got out of bed. I grabbed a sweatshirt from the hook on the back of the door and pulled it over my head. The living room was pitch black, and I flipped on the kitchen light. Randolph swam happily around in his home, not caring that it was the middle of the night. I wrapped my arms around my waist and stood still, listening for the noise, anxiety crept up my back. There was a smell. It took me a few seconds to realize what it was…smoke.

"Tate!" I ran back to the bedroom and flipped the light on. She was sitting up, the covers thrown back. "There's smoke!" I grabbed my sweatpants off the floor and yanked them on.

"Where?" She climbed out of bed and snatched her T-shirt from the chair.

"I'm not sure. I smelled it in the living room." I pushed my feet into tennis shoes I hadn't untied.

Tate pulled on her pants and shoes and grabbed her phone. I grabbed mine off the nightstand, and we hurried to the living room. Smoke was making its way under the front door. I grabbed Randolph's bowl and yelled to Tate, "The bedroom window! There's a roll-up ladder under the bed!"

Tate grabbed the quilt off the couch and shoved it up against the bottom of the door, then we ran back to the bedroom just as the smoke alarm started screaming. Tate knelt beside the bed, pulled out a bundle of ropes and metal hooks, and looked at me.

"Mike got it in case there was an emergency." I set Randolph on the nightstand and opened the window.

"Remind me to give that queen a kiss." She dropped one end out the window and hung the hooks on the windowsill. "You first. I'll carry Randolph down."

I threw one leg over the windowsill, then the other, and started down, one rung at a time. When I reached the bottom, I found my phone and dialed 911. Tate climbed out using one hand, clutching Randolph tightly to her chest with the other. It took a little longer for her to reach the ground since she was one-handing it, but she made it. She handed Randolph to me. He swam around, unfazed by the danger he'd been in. I set him on the ground and wrapped my arms around Tate, squeezing her so tight she might not have been able to breathe.

"The fire department's on the way. We're okay," I reassured her.

The smoke in the air burned my eyes as we hurried to the front of the garage and peered around the corner to the staircase. The porch light was out. It's on a timer set to come on at dusk. Tate had replaced the bulb for me a week ago, so it had to have been intentionally disabled. Fire glowed at the top of the stairs. Someone had piled flattened cardboard boxes several feet high in front of the door. The fire had consumed most of it but hadn't caught the door on fire.

"Shit!" Tate grabbed my hand.

"What?" I looked around.

"It's a trap. He smoked us out." She pulled me away from the garage. We'd only taken two steps when a figure in black jumped out of the shadows and blocked our path. I froze. It was Max. Even in the darkness I could see the scars on his arm glisten. The rage on his face twisted it into something out of a horror movie. He grabbed my arm, squeezing so hard his fingernails pierced my skin. Hate radiated off him. "I'm going to kill you, bitch." Spit flew from his mouth.

Tate charged him and he slapped her away like a bug. She flew backward, hitting the ground. She lay there unmoving.

"Tate!" I screamed and tried to pull away, but he jerked me around, nearly dislocating my shoulder. I fell to my knees in pain.

"You're coming with me, cunt." He dragged me toward the street but before he'd gotten very far, Tate launched herself at him from behind and clung to his back like a tick on a dog. He stumbled, letting go of my arm and throwing Tate off.

"Run," she yelled, getting to her feet as he turned around and lurched for her. Tate ducked out of his grasp and kicked him in the balls. I'd say he screamed like a little girl, but that would be an insult to little girls everywhere.

He grabbed his crotch with both hands, his knees buckled, and he collapsed to the ground, rolling from side to side. I scooped up Randolph and we took off running. I looked over my shoulder to see Max trying to get to his feet.

"I'll kill you, bitch!"

For a guy who'd just had his family jewels crushed, he could still yell pretty loud. As I ran I clasped Randolph's bowl to my chest with one hand and covered the opening at the top with the other to keep him from bouncing out. It slowed me down. Behind us I heard Max curse as he pushed himself to his feet and started after us. What would he do if he caught us? Did he have a weapon? Tate and I were unarmed, we hadn't had time to retrieve our weapons from the gun safe. We ran down the middle of the street. Blood pounded in my ears, and my lungs burned. I thought I was in better shape than this. I was really going to have to get to the gym more.

The street behind us lit up, and the roar of a car engine raced toward us. I looked over my shoulder just as a black Ford Taurus with tinted windows hit Max from behind. It was like watching a movie in slow motion as he bounced onto the hood, and then the windshield, then over the top, and somersaulted off the trunk. There was a flash of pink in the driver's seat. Pinky. She didn't stop and the car sped off into the darkness.

I stood frozen, my mouth open, no words coming out. Max lay sprawled on the street not moving. My stomach lurched at the sight of his arms and legs twisted at odd angles, blood oozing from his ears and nose. I gagged and almost threw up but swallowed it down.

I looked at Tate. "Is he dead?"

She walked over to him, knelt and placed her fingertips on his neck. She looked back at me. "He's breathing and there's a heartbeat." She took her phone out and called 911. "This is Detective Walker. We'll need police and an ambulance to respond to the fire on Albert Drive." She gave them some additional information and disconnected.

"Did you see who was driving?" She searched my face.

I stared into her eyes and shook my head. "No," I lied. "It's dark. There's no streetlight."

"I didn't either. It happened so fast."

I couldn't tell if she was lying or if she really didn't see Pinky in the driver's seat.

"I didn't see the license plate. Did you?" she asked.

I shook my head. "I don't think there was one."

"Probably stolen." She hugged Randolph and me to her. "I doubt we'll ever catch who did it."

I pulled back just enough to look up at her. "Just as well, I suppose."

She nodded and hugged us tighter.

The fire department finally left at four in the morning. Detectives Cup and Skylar, looking like they'd dragged themselves out of bed, took our statements. They didn't question us further about not seeing the driver or the license plate.

Luckily the damage to my apartment was minimal. The screen door was a total loss and the front door might have to be replaced, but thanks to Tate's quick thinking with the quilt under the door, there wasn't a lot of smoke damage inside. It would need several days to air out, though. Tate insisted I stay with her, so I grabbed a change of clothes and Randolph's food from the kitchen drawer. To be safe, I grabbed the spare key, and the three of us went to Tate's for a few hours of sleep.

When the sun rose later, Tate was still in bed beside me, her arm protectively wrapped around my naked midsection, her breasts pressed against my back. She mumbled when I scooted to the edge of the bed and reached into my pants on the floor. I rolled back over and faced her. Her eyes were open and she was smiling.

"Good morning," I said.

"I like waking up with you in my bed."

"I like it too." I cuddled up next to her and rested my head on her chest.

"We should talk about last night," she said.

"Which part? Max almost killing us? Or Max being laid out on the pavement by a hit-and-run driver?"

"The hit-and-run driver." She rolled onto her side facing me. "You know who it was, don't you?" It wasn't really a question.

I nodded. "Are you okay letting her get away with it? I mean she did save both of our lives."

She blew out her breath. "I didn't see anything. Period."

"Okay." I held out my hand in front of her, fist closed. "Open it."

Her eyebrows scrunched together. "A present for me?"

I grinned. "A long overdue present."

She sat up and opened my hand with both of hers. Inside was my spare key.

Her face lit up. "Is this to your apartment?"

I nodded. "You don't have to knock anymore. Just walk in whenever you want." I wasn't ready to give up my apartment, but I was ready to take this step.

She took the key. "You're sure?"

"I'm sure."

"What about the FBI?"

"I'm rethinking that."

"Really?"

I nodded. "Really."

She wrapped her arms around me and squeezed me to her.

I pulled back and in all seriousness said, "There's just one condition."

She crossed her arms over her chest in mock indignation. "There's always a catch."

I laughed. "If anything happens to me, you have to promise to take care of Randolph."

"You know I would never let anything happen to you or Randolph," she said as she leaned in and captured my lips with hers.

EPILOGUE

It had been almost a year since Max set fire to my apartment and tried to kill us. Since then, our lives had settled into a routine, splitting nights between my place and Tate's. Even after all this time, and all we'd been through, I still wasn't ready to settle down into domestic bliss, much to my mother's disappointment.

The authorities charged Max with several counts of attempted murder for the fires at the pub and multiple counts of arson for the fires he set around town, including my apartment. His trial was coming up in a month. Thankfully, the court denied him bail because of his having spectacularly violated parole. He'd been in jail following his three-week stay in the hospital. His injuries included two broken legs, a broken arm, collarbone, and several ribs, one of which punctured a lung.

Pinky called the day after the incident to tell me she was going to Mexico. I managed to talk her out of it. Leaving the country, or even the state, would violate her probation and she didn't need another warrant out for her arrest. Since then, she'd been on her best behavior. At least as far as I knew. Since her arrest warrant had been quashed, she was no longer my responsibility. I tried my best not to ask her new probation officer how she was doing. I was probably better off not knowing.

Six months ago Tate was promoted to sergeant and put in charge of the motorcycle unit. It meant she was back to wearing those form-fitting pants and the knee-high boots she'd been wearing the day she'd pulled me over all those years ago. She was happy as a clam to be back chasing down speeders and red-light runners, and I was happy looking at her ass in her new uniform.

I was still in the warrant apprehension unit, tracking down rogue probationers and doing my best to stay out of Stan's crosshairs and in his good graces. It was a tightrope walk every day.

This week we were staying at my apartment, Randolph felt more at home there. With Tate on the two-to-ten shift, I had the place to myself for the evening. After a cheese and tomato sandwich, I remembered I'd put a load of clothes in the dryer before I left that morning. I retrieved them, folded them, and went to the bedroom to put them away. I'd made space for Tate to hang a few things in my closet and emptied two drawers in the dresser. I figured any more than that sent the wrong message.

I opened one of Tate's drawers to put her socks away and noticed a small black object peeking out from under a pair of lace panties. Of course, my curiosity peaked, so I nudged it out from under the panties. A very small black square box glared up at me. Only one thing came in that kind of box, and it wasn't a puppy. I didn't know whether to be angry or afraid. Angry because Tate knew I didn't want to get married, or afraid because she might actually ask me to marry her. I shoved the offending object back under the panties and closed the drawer. Maybe it would go away if I ignored it.

I stalked to the kitchen to retrieve a beer from the refrigerator. I plopped myself on the couch, crossed one leg over the other, guzzled down half the beer and watched my foot bob up and down. What the hell was I going to do? I wasn't ready for that kind of commitment.

After agonizing over my predicament for the better part of three hours, I marched into the bedroom, snatched the damn little box out of Tate's drawer, and returned to the couch to await Tate's arrival. Thirty minutes later I heard her key in the door, and she walked in looking beat. For a second I thought about waiting to confront her, but I was too keyed up to let it go.

"Hi, babe." She dropped her gym bag next to the door and walked toward me. She paused when she noticed my arms crossed and my furrowed brow. "Is everything okay?"

"I don't know, is it?"

"Ummm, I'm not sure what's going on here." Her eyes darted to the right, then to the left.

"What's this?" I brandished the little box like a weapon.

Tate's entire demeanor relaxed, and the corners of her mouth raised in a mischievous grin. "It looks like a tiny black box. What's it look like to you?"

She was enjoying my discomfort. "It looks like a ring box."

She nodded. "Yeah, that's what it looks like to me too." Her grin grew bigger.

I could feel my face getting red. There was nothing funny about an engagement ring.

She lifted an eyebrow and took the box from me. "Where did you find it?"

I refolded my arms across my chest. "In your sock drawer."

She cocked her head. "So you were going through my drawer?"

"No." I shook my head. "No, I was putting clothes away and it was right there."

She nodded, the grin returning. She opened the box and held it out for me to see. The ring was silver with a square-cut diamond that sparkled in the light. "It's pretty, don't you think?"

I shrugged.

"But it's not really your style, is it?"

I looked from the ring to her face. What kind of game was she playing?

"No," I said hesitantly. "I'm not really a diamond kind of girl."

As she closed the lid to the box, she chuckled and sat beside me. "Riley, I know you don't like diamonds, so I would never buy you a diamond engagement ring."

My head spun. What was going on here? Why did she have an engagement ring if it wasn't for me? "So why do you have an engagement ring in your sock drawer?"

She set the box on the coffee table. "Remember Frank?"

"The guy on the bomb squad?"

"Yeah, that guy." She grinned. "He's going to propose to his girlfriend. He asked me to keep it until Saturday, so she didn't find it and ruin the surprise."

I let out a sigh, part relief, part embarrassment.

She leaned in and kissed my cheek. "If, and when the day comes, I promise it won't be a diamond ring hidden in a sock drawer."

I chuckled, feeling the weight lift off my shoulders. "Good to know."

She stood. "I'm going to jump in the shower." She pulled her sweatshirt over her shoulders. She wasn't wearing a bra. Her mischievous grin returned. She winked at me and raised an eyebrow. "Care to join me?"

I sprang off the couch. "Last one in's a rotten egg," I laughed, pulling my own shirt off as I sprinted down the hall.

Bella Books, Inc.

Happy Endings Live Here

P.O. Box 10543
Tallahassee, FL 32302
Phone: (850) 576-2370
www.BellaBooks.com

More Titles from Bella Books

Hunter's Revenge – Gerri Hill
978-1-64247-447-3 | 276 pgs | paperback: $18.95 | eBook: $9.99
Tori Hunter is back! Don't miss this final chapter in the acclaimed Tori Hunter series.

Integrity – E. J. Noyes
978-1-64247-465-7 | 228 pgs | paperback: $19.95 | eBook: $9.99
It was supposed to be an ordinary workday...

The Order – TJ O'Shea
978-1-64247-378-0 | 396 pgs | paperback: $19.95 | eBook: $9.99
For two women the battle between new love and old loyalty may prove more dangerous than the war they're trying to survive.

Under the Stars with You – Jaime Clevenger
978-1-64247-439-8 | 302 pgs | paperback: $19.95 | eBook: $9.99
Sometimes believing in love is the first step. And sometimes it's all about trusting the stars.

The Missing Piece – Kat Jackson
978-1-64247-445-9 | 250 pgs | paperback: $18.95 | eBook: $9.99
Renee's world collides with possibility and the past, setting off a tidal wave of changes she could have never predicted.

An Acquired Taste – Cheri Ritz
978-1-64247-462-6 | 206 pgs | paperback: $17.95 | eBook: $9.99
Can Elle and Ashley stand the heat in the *Celebrity Cook Off* kitchen?

Printed in the USA
CPSIA information can be obtained
at www.ICGtesting.com
JSHW020214081224
75010JS00001B/2

9 781642 476200